Sophia's CONNECTION

A TWIN FLAME NOVEL

GRACEN MILLER

BAMA GIRL PRESS, LLC

The unauthorized reproduction or distribution of this copyrighted work is illegal. Criminal copyright infringement (including infringement without monetary gain) is investigated by the FBI and is punishable by up to 5 years in federal prison and a fine of $250,000.

This book is a work of fiction. Names, characters, places, and incidents are the products of the author's imagination or used fictitiously. Any resemblance to actual events, locales or persons, living or dead, is entirely coincidental.

Sophia's Connection
Copyright © 2019 by Gracen Miller
Published by Bama Girl Press, LLC
Cover art designed by Brannon Jones at B Creative Designs
All photos for cover art were purchased through Shutterstock

All rights reserved. Except for use in any review, the reproduction or utilization of this work, in whole or in part, in any form by any electronic, mechanical or other means now known or hereafter invented, is forbidden without the written permission of the publisher.

Manufactured in the United States.

Scandalous plot? Random coincidence? Or destiny's design?

Born to the camp whore, Sinner Prometheus grew up hard. Trench was sold into slavery by his mother for the price of a meal. Their tragedies united them, and they fought for their freedom. One act of piracy united them with Leopold, the son of an intergalactic senator. United by a destiny few understand, their dynamic family thrives on love, power, and trust. They've built an empire that caters to the sins of others where they rule with an iron fist. They're feared and respected, rarely defied, and living the dream.

In polite society, Sophia Thornrose is whispered about among her peers, but never publicly ridiculed because of her aristocratic family. She's a freak who sees the dead and has a spirit sidekick that never shuts up. Despite her scandalous peculiarity, she's sought by eligible bachelors, but she craves more from life than a mundane marriage and children. She wants adventure and equality, to be loved for her oddity.

When Sinner takes a gig to assassinate Sophia, Trench and Leopold go along for the ride. None of them knew their life missed a key component until Sinner kidnaps Sophia.

A chance moment, a destiny they can't see coming, it'll be the ride of their.

DEDICATION

For all those who daydream about an alternate reality. Never stop dreaming!

ONE

Sinner

I can't believe I'm about to kill an innocent woman.

Sinner Prometheus had also flown his spaceship across four universes to this godforsaken planet to get the job done. What could he say? He was bored and the pay was good.

Located in the Jaguar solar system on the planet Uriel, the people were uptight, outdated, and living in a male hierarchy run system. Women everywhere should rise up and demand equal rights. Several women he knew could fuck a man up without batting an eyelash.

Sighing, Sinner shook his head.

Not my problem.

He wasn't even sure why he'd taken the goddamn job. It wasn't like he needed the money. Boredom affected men in strange ways. But Uriel added a new layer to his disinterest.

Through the balcony window he scoffed at the twits dancing about the ballroom. In no mood to entertain, he stepped outside to escape the frivolous party.

Teenage girls vying to win the hand of the most eligible bachelor, oftentimes their grandfather's age, disgusted him. He ran a planet based off desires, even the taboo ones, but the Uriel girls were pawned off to men as if they held no other value to a family other than the title of the man they could snag.

Shaking his head, Sinner lit an e-cig and inhaled the plant based stimulant. Thankfully the shadows of the balcony cloaked his presence.

A few minutes later, a woman stepped onto the balcony. Even with her features obstructed by the domino covering the top part of her face, he identified her as Sophia Thornrose. The Duke of Redesdale's daughter and his host for tonight's soiree.

And the one I've been paid to assassinate.

Sinner had done his homework on his mark. Sophia was a legend among polite society at breaking hearts. Gossip held that if her ghostly sidekick—Sin shook his head at that lunacy—didn't like a suitor, he was kicked out the door without a backward glance. Among her peers she was thought to be insane, but her daddy had more money than their king, so they tolerated her madness and vied for her hand in marriage.

Ridiculous. Spineless fucktards.

Although Sophia *was* without question beautiful, her beauty wasn't enough to endure her eccentricity. He'd take an ugly, kinky bitch to his bed over the handful the Duke's daughter would bring to a man's life.

SOPHIA'S CONNECTION

One look at her face inspired him to tow his husbands across galaxies to kill her. There was something about her that hit him square in the gut. He didn't like it.

Shaking that off he thought about the details he'd learned about her since landing on Uriel. Word on the street labeled her eccentric, sweet, and gentle hearted, but a possessor of dark magic. Fraud or legitimate, she earned a damn good living as a medium. An anomaly in her male driven society. That ambition he respected.

What he couldn't figure out was why someone wanted her dead. She seemed harmless enough to him. Because of her planet's idiotic rule that all unmarried women must have a chaperone when in the presence of a male, he'd anticipated having to maneuver heaven and earth to get her alone so he could snap her neck.

Instead, she came to me.

As Sophia walked to the balustrade, she ripped her domino off and tossed it on the floor. She hiked her skirt to the bottom swell of her ass. Sinner admired the show of flesh until he realized she planned to go *over* the railing. It was at least a thirty-foot drop. If the fall didn't kill her, she would suffer broken bones at the very least.

Sinner stepped from the shadows. "*Stop!*"

She jerked her head up at the sound of his voice and lost her grip on the bannister. Losing her balance, she toppled to the right, on a direct plunge to her possible death. Sinner leapt forward and caught her arm before her graceless swan dive. He dragged her over the balustrade to safe footing and she hissed at him. Amidst copious quantities of soft woman and ridiculous amounts of fabric, he hauled her to her feet and steadied her with his hands on her shoulders.

"You're welcome," he said, his tone dry.

"You fool!" She tilted her head back and glared at him.

Her scent electrified him and for a moment the world faded away. A familiar burn stung his wrist.

"You could've killed me," she snarled.

Not that he expected any thanks from a suicidal woman, but a little respect would be nice. "*You* were the one jumping. I saved you." Why had he saved her ass when she could've done his job for him and broken her neck without him lifting a finger. The hit *was* supposed to look like an accident. "I repeat… you're welcome."

"Imbecile." Sophia snorted.

A delightful noise one of her status should never make in the presence of others. Charmed by the indelicate sound, Sinner bit back a grin. She rolled her shoulders, a silent hint for him to release her. He complied, elevating his hands to indicate he freed her of his hold. A wise man would break her neck before tipping her over the railing, creating neat evidence for suicide.

That tingle on his wrist held him back. With two twin flames waiting for him on his ship, he couldn't risk losing a third. Although finding another flame was highly unlikely, he couldn't chance it.

Before lowering his hands, he tugged up the sleeve on his dinner jacket to peek at the inside of his arm. In the dim balcony lighting, he couldn't discern a new mark, but he chose to err on the side of caution.

Sophia patted at her intricate hair design and rubbed her left wrist against her skirt. At her move, his gut clenched.

Fucking Christ. She had to be a twin flame.

"You thought I planned to jump to my death?" She rolled her eyes at him.

What had she expected him to think when she attempted to climb over the railing?

He lifted his hand to finger a blonde glossy ringlet but froze with his hand in midair when he realized his intentions.

I've lost my goddamn mind.

He lowered his arm and didn't give a damn if she noticed his slight. "What else was I to think when you climbed over the railing? What exactly had you planned?"

She put some distance between them and settled on the edge of the bench. Odd since the seat placed her in shadows. Remaining alone with a man that wasn't her husband was ill advised on her backward world, where women were doted upon, and treated like inferior, brainless creatures. Some of the most calculating and intelligent minds he knew belonged to women.

Had she been any other woman, he'd have thought she sought to snag him as a spouse. Then again no one could force his hand, not even her high-ranking parent. Despite his appearance and credentials of a titled lord, he off-worlder status meant he was untouchable by their customs.

Her shoulders stiffened and her spine snapped a little straighter. As she turned her head aside, he thought the word 'no' slid past her lips. To whom did she speak? Her so-called ghostly guardian he'd heard rumors about?

Sinner strode to the balustrade and angled his stance so he could lean against the railing. He made no attempt to hide his gaze on her person. With his countenance cloaked in the shadows, she'd be able to sense his stare at the very least, while his view of her remained unobstructed. The gas lamp cast enough light to showcase her features.

"There's a ledge on the other side and a hidden door that leads to a stairwell to the roof."

Nonplussed by her comment, he coolly studied her. "Pardon?"

"You asked why I climbed the balustrade. I'm attempting to explain. Stairwell to the roof." The final sentence came out slowly as if she explained herself to a numbskull. Sophia pointed upward as a soft, fatigued sigh emerged. His dick took inappropriate notice.

What the hell was wrong with him? Only loose women interested him. They came with no strings attached and were not virgins—what idiot wanted a virgin anyway? Regardless, he couldn't help but wonder if she'd make the same noise when he was inside her.

SOPHIA'S CONNECTION

If she's a twin flame, I'll take her anyway I can get her. Only a damn fool walked away from a twin flame. Sinner was no fool.

She sent a sidelong glance to her right. The same direction she'd peered earlier when she uttered 'no'. He couldn't be certain, but he thought her features tightened for a fraction of a second as if passing along silent communication with another. Only no one else was present.

Is the girl as mad as everyone claims?

Even knowing the rumors had not prepared him for watching her engage with an undetectable individual.

A moment later, she tilted her head and gazed in his direction. The pinch of her mouth evidenced her irritation. But at whom? "There were too many ghosts inside. Pretending we are alone, while maintaining a smile sometimes grows tedious. I desired a moment of solitude."

Her eyes were light in color, but he couldn't discern their exact shade in the sconce's soft glow. The picture he'd been given when hired to eliminate her had been in black and white. He shouldn't care about their color at all since she *had* to die, and he never failed at a job. Yet he'd be lying if he pretended he wasn't interested in her.

"A lady of your stature should not be unattended."

She shook her head. "You men think you know what's best for a woman."

The inclination to place his mouth against hers to erase her frown resulted in a smile corrupting his. He bet the girl had never been kissed properly. If at all. He shifted his stance. That she was untrained in the arts of sex should've cooled his ardor, instead her chastity increased his discomfort.

"Ladies do not always prefer entertainment to privacy. At least not this lady."

It took Sin a moment to recall their prior comments. "Sophia—"

"I didn't grant you liberty to use my name." Her mouth remained parted as if his forwardness shocked her.

"I took the liberty."

"Have we met?"

He crossed an ankle over the other, leaned his elbow on the rail, and gave her his identity for this planet—a self-indulgent namesake. "Chalmers Wentworth."

"Ah…the reclusive Earl of Huntingdon. A mystery in polite society and highly sought after by stupid maidens everywhere." She sounded bored and unimpressed by the title he'd stolen from the deceased Earl. Then again her father was a Duke, and sixth in line for the crown.

Sin snorted at her obvious sarcasm for 'stupid maidens'. "I'm surprised you know of me."

"I know all my father's cronies by name."

"I'm not the Duke's crony."

Sophia shrugged as if his association with her father mattered little to her. She shot a distinct irritated glance to her right once more. The girl's oddity increased his curiosity.

"Acquaintance then." She faced him once more, elevating her eyebrows. "I thought you were older."

Sin laughed. "Does your father approve of your trysts atop the battlements?"

She brought danger to herself by climbing the guardrail in the bundle of skirts she wore for no other purpose than to gain entry to a hidden doorway.

Then again... *she's my goddamn target.*

"If he knew, I'd talk him out of his anger."

Spoiled. "He should spank your ass for your insolence." He wanted to lay his hand on her backside too, but to see to her pleasure rather than her punishment. "I'd use my hand."

"I beg your pardon?"

Unaware he spoke aloud until her scandalized tenor penetrated his fantasy, he decided in an instant there'd be no point in trying to save face now. He'd wing it. The lighting slanted at the correct angle that he could just make out the darkening on her cheeks. A pity he couldn't detect the flush in proper lighting.

How far will that blush go?

He bet the flush would spread far enough her breasts would grow rosy. His dick hardened painfully. Good thing she didn't look down or the evidence of his arousal would be obvious.

I could fuck her before I kill her.

Wouldn't be the worst crime he'd ever committed.

Pretty damn sure I can't kill her either.

"One slip like tonight and you'd be broken on the lawn below."

"You were the fault of that near miss." Her haughty attitude rankled him.

Sinner shoved away from the railing and walked toward her until he pressed his boots to her hemline. Someone should scare her from her outrageous behavior. Why he felt obligated to be the one was beyond him when he preferred his women ballsy. On her planet, that type of behavior got a girl killed. "A couple stealing a kiss might've allowed you to fall to hide their misdeeds. So, yes, I'd use my hand on your ass. First, I'd put you over my knees, lift your skirts and expose your—"

"*Lord Huntingdon!*" She leapt to her feet. "This conversation is scandalous."

No idea what he planned, he caught her by her arms before she could flounce away. "That you're alone with *me* is enough to be scandal worthy."

Her breath hitched when he shifted his right hand and slid it up her arm to graze across her collarbone. Perversion continued the caress, along her throat to where her pulse beat in erratic thumps against the pad of his thumb.

Sophia isn't immune to me.

That achievement should alarm him, but rather than dispel his passion his cock hardened to the point of pain and his trousers chafed his arousal.

"Fred, do not," she muttered.

Fred? The misspoken name resulted in the same effect as ice water being tossed on his crotch. "Who the fuck is Fred?"

A flash of panic contorted her features.

"I should go now bef—" She gasped before going tense in his arms.

"Sophia?"

Her countenance blanked and her eyes darkened to brown. It was as if she became a different person altogether. It went down as one of the strangest fucking things he'd ever seen.

"Your mission is not worth all you've worked for, your life or that of your partners," her voice emerged devoid of any emotion and tinged with a deeper quality, like a man. "Take heed, without your twin flame you will lose all you've gained."

A chill swept down his spine. How could Sophia know of his mission? He knew for a fact that the legend of twin flames was not a commonly known folktale on Uriel.

Sinner yanked his hands off her. "Who are you?"

"Fred." Sophia smirked, but it twisted his gut in the wrong way. "You can thank me later," 'Fred' said.

The seizure that assailed her next surprised him and she went boneless. Gravity took over and Sinner caught her before she hit the floor, but just barely. He swung her into his arms with the realization that she had to be another twin flame. That he already had two others didn't matter to him.

I have to get her to safety and fast.

"Thanks for knocking her out, Fred."

TWO

Sophia

Sophia came awake seated in Lord Huntingdon's lap. It was highly inappropriate, but the man was attractive with his blonde hair and brown eyes.

"What'd I say?" She knew exactly what Fred made her say.

The jerk.

"Nice ruse. I'm not buying it."

"No ruse, Lord Huntingdon. When Fred takes me over—*what* are you doing?"

He untied his cravat and she gaped at him. The illicit idea of him undressing teased her core and left her clit buzzing.

"Tending to business, Sophia." His no-nonsense tone left her stomach fluttering.

She should've reacted, but she was too fascinated watching him work the knot out. Her prior lovers had come to her bed quickly and unwilling to undress fully for fear her father would discover them.

Uriel government forbid women to engage in sex, but that hadn't stopped Sophia. She knew too much about sex thanks to Fred, and she'd been interested. She'd discovered she had needs just like a man.

I'm wanton.

But she didn't care what Uriel men thought of her. Even as a child she'd known she was destined for another planet, another world with a different way of thinking, and with more than one man as her lover.

Fred had warned her to maintain her silence or risk censure or death.

She'd begun to worry Fred lied, until he used her mouth to call Lord Huntingdon her twin flame.

"Is he really one of them?" she asked Fred. He looked normal, nothing like what she expected an alien from another planet to look like.

The ghostly apparition nodded. "He's not what I expected either."

Fred could say that again.

"Is who one of what?" Lord Huntingdon asked.

"I was talking to Fred."

He met her gaze as he tugged the tie free of his neck. The sensual move escalated her heartbeat and dampness pooled between her thighs.

"Give me your wrists."

"Why?"

Lord Huntingdon drew her hands together. "I'm taking you to the Prometheus Solar system where the planet I own is located."

"You're an alien?" She felt her eyes widen at that because he didn't look alien.

His mouth parted and he halted with his tie roped around her wrist. "Alien isn't the PC terminology."

"What's PC?"

"Politically correct." He went back to wrapping her wrists and binding her with his cravat. "You know there's life on other planets?"

"Fred tells me a lot." She'd be fighting him to the death right now if Fred hadn't called him her twin.

"Back to that bullshit, huh?" He shook his head.

"You don't believe I can talk to the dead?"

"Sure, mediums probably exist but few are real." He shrugged. "Most are charlatans looking for easy money. I know. I employ several. I don't really give a fuck which one you are, just don't expect me to fall for your shit."

"You're the jaded one." One man would be a jaded assassin, another a warrior, and the last a politician. All of them feared by others because of their power. "The one sent to kill me."

His gaze snapped to hers.

Lord Huntingdon's wide-eyed gape let her know she'd shocked him with her knowledge. She lifted one shoulder in a shrug. "Told you Fred tells me a lot."

"Atlantis—that's my planet—caters to sins and vices of all nature." With a finger hooked around the knot about her wrists, he tugged her closer to his chest. "I've decided not to kill you yet. I have a fancy to teach you every one of those depravities before I get rid of you?"

His threat would've terrified the average Uriel woman. Instead he promised something she'd craved for a long time. Freedom to be herself, to express her desires, and escape this patriarchal planet. Thanks to her spirit sidekick she knew there were dozens of other planets with different forms of life. A lot of them more advanced than her world. And while the Earl was humanoid, not all were.

Lord Huntingdon also wasn't the only person who'd been sent to kill her. The first attempt was a month ago, the second just last week. They both rotted in a prison in her father's cellar while he thought up ways to torture information out of them. No closer to the truth of who hired them, maybe the Earl would have more information.

"Who hired you to kill me?"

"Don't know."

"How many people have you killed?"

"A lot."

She bit the inside of her cheek. That should disgust her not send a shiver of desire along her body.

"Does that frighten you?" His salacious smile set her heart to pounding.

He was good-looking enough with his pale hair. A lot of the single ladies swooned over him earlier in the night, but she hadn't pegged him as her type. "You're proud of your kill count?"

"I'm an intergalactic assassin, Sophia." He touched her mouth with his fingertip, and she parted her lips. "If I don't boast my own accomplishments, no one will."

"Do you murder children too?" She held her breath as she awaited his reply.

"You're a snob."

"I'm... yeah, I am." She bit his finger and he yanked it back. "It keeps people away. What's your excuse for being a bastard?"

The Earl chuckled right. "That the best slur you have?"

Her nipples tingled at his husky laugh and that irritated her. He hadn't answered her question and *that* frightened her. If children were not off limit targets, then wouldn't he have come right out and said so?

Sophia used her bound hands on his chest to balance herself as she slid off his lap. She had to put some distance between them so she could think. Could she be happy with a child killer?

"I don't know if I can do this," she muttered to herself.

"If you don't you'll die in the next month," Fred said.

"I assassinate, not murder." The Earl pinned her against the rail, his breath hitting the back of her ear. "It's a classier distinction."

She snorted. "Pardon me if it doesn't feel classier."

"If you're life has value, you're assassinated. If you don't matter, you're murdered. Someone thinks your life has value, Sophia, and he or she paid me a fuckton of money to take you out."

"That's not his real looks," Fred said out of the clear blue while tapping his chin. He studied Lord Huntingdon, sizing him up. "You'll still like his real look. He's definitely one of yours. And you *have* to go with him."

Sophia glared at the spirit. "Shut. Up."

"You won't get an apology from me. The truth hurts, doll," Lord Huntingdon growled against her ear.

"That was for Fred."

"Does Fred often interfere with your conversations?"

"Not often. He implied your appearance was a façade."

"Oh, it is." He turned her to face him and lifted his jacket to show her a serious of round colored designs painted onto his forearm. "Each of these are implants for different functions. The black one alters my appearance. Can't take the risk of assassinating—"

"Murdering."

"—someone with my real face." He sighed. "You're having a problem differentiating between the two, aren't you?"

"You would as well if it was your life."

"Touché."

"Release me and I'll double whatever you were paid." Bargaining wouldn't work, but she couldn't take the chance he didn't know she was meant for him.

"Decline. I don't need the money. I do it for fun."

"Fun?" She wet her lips and looked away. That confession bothered her a little. Killing shouldn't be fun.

"That's all true, but he knows you belong to him," Fred's comment jerked her gaze back to the Earl. Hope set her heartbeat to racing.

"I'll get Fred to divulge whatever you want to know about your future," she offered.

"That's a lie," Fred drawled. "I won't tell him anything until you're on his ship and on your way to his planet."

Lord Huntingdon didn't know that though.

"What's Fred going to tell me that I don't already know?" The Earl shook his head at her as if disappointed with her bargaining skills. "I already know I'm fucking awesome."

"True." Fred nodded. "He is. You'll find out soon enough"

Without thought, she reacted and snarled at Fred. "If I could crush your windpipe, I would."

Fred gave a boyish grin, the same one she always received when he agitated her. He wasn't nearly as charming as he thought he was though.

"That was hot." The Earl tucked locks of her hair behind one of her ears. "I like a woman with spunk."

"Lord Huntingdon—"

"Sinner."

Confused she frowned. "Huh?"

"My name is Sinner Prometheus."

He'd said the solar system his planet resided in was named Prometheus. Nothing narcissistic about naming yourself after a universe. "You must be proud."

"Everyone calls me Sinner. I am proud. It's a name that puts fear into people." He removed a handkerchief from his breast pocket. "Enough talk, we have a spaceship to catch."

Sophia bolted for the door because she felt it was expected of her. Wouldn't he question if she didn't attempt an escape?

He yanked her away from the door and shoved a handkerchief into her mouth before she could scream.

"Pathetic try."

For that comment, she managed enough movement to knee him in the crotch. He went down but took her with him.

"Fuck," he snarled in her face as he released her arm and his fingers slid into her hair. His grip tightened on her strands until her scalp stung. "You can kiss it all better later."

She tried to say, "No way in hell," but it came out so messed up even she couldn't understand her words.

Sinner chuckled and rubbed his penis with his other hand. "You're glorious when you're angry."

That actually pissed her off. His eyes widened and he went into action. He stood and yanked her up with him. She squealed when he hauled her over his shoulder. Her belly took the brunt of the impact and air whooshed from her lungs.

"Move too much and we'll both fall to our deaths." He followed his warning with a swat to her bottom, not that she felt much more than a pat thanks to her layers of clothing.

Did he plan to climb the railing and shimmy down the bannister *with her in his arms*?

Scrunching her eyes closed, she buried her face against Sinner's back and clutched at his clothing to balance herself. Death might not scare her, but she held no desire to see it coming. What felt like an eternity of descent, they finally touched the earth and he strode deeper into the gardens with her.

Sophia had no idea how long Sinner walked until he set her on her feet, ripped a length of material off her skirts and blindfolded her. She flinched when she felt his fingertip run along her jaw.

"Trussed up, gagged, and blindfolded." His lips touched her ear. Her breath hitched at the illicit excitement that eddied through her belly in a flash of heat and wetness between her thighs. "Helpless. At my mercy."

The eroticism of his mouth moving against her lobe scattered goose bumps along her skin. His breath panted suggestively, and her nipples responded, growing tight and achy. Hands grasped her shoulders as he sucked her earlobe into his mouth, his tongue licking and biting along the shell. The sting erotic in a way she would've never imagined possible.

At the moment, she didn't feel helpless, but enchanted by his sway and desire rushed through in her a wave of heat. Breath catching, she jerked away from him because of how powerful her yearning felt.

"That's my darkest fantasy right there," the husky drawl to his voice inflamed her senses and she melted against him once again.

Even though her lust felt out of control, she yearned for his touch also.

Fingertips skimmed her cheekbone, slid along her nose and circled her lips. "I'd make you come over and over again before I thrust my dick inside you." She tried to shake her head because the visual left her mouth dry with longing, but his hand shifted to her throat and squeezed just enough to halt her protest. "It'll happen. Accept the outcome and you'll enjoy it." *He is* no *gentleman.* Geez that excited her even more. "The prevalent inquiry is who'll claim you first. Me, Trench or Leopold?"

She guessed those were the name of her other men. He swung her into his arms, and she hooked her bound wrists over his neck.

"You wanted adventure," Fred's dry tone irritated her. "It's knocking on your door like I told you it would."

Shut up, she screeched behind the gag.

"Can't understand you, love." By the swift gait they traveled, she determined Sinner's stride was quick. "Save your energy for later."

Later? What'd he have planned for later?

"Seduction, my dear girl. Your seduction is in the future."

THREE
Trench

"Interesting choice of décor," Trench remarked when Sinner entered the den of their spacecraft with a woman over his shoulder.

"She doesn't fit the current motif," Leopold drawled while he poured a finger of dragon venom, a stout liquor made popular on Atlantis for its dragon enhancement.

Sinner set Sophia on her feet and she stepped back into Sinner's space, as if he offered protection rather than her recent kidnapping.

Trench rose to his feet and approached Sinner. "I always did prefer blondes."

The woman squeezed a little tighter against her captor and Sinner mocked her with a snicker. She twisted her body so she could elbow Sinner in the gut, and of course he chuckled at her violence.

"She's a gift for us." Sinner jerked off his ridiculous jacket, yanked up his sleeve, and lifted his arm. On his wrist a third twin flame mark had appeared. "As you can tell, she clearly doesn't comprehend she should stop fighting back."

Seeing the third twin flame mark on Sinner's wrist made Trench realize he rubbed at a sudden sting on his skin. He looked at his flesh where a third mark had appeared above his other two. The first two he shared with Sinner and Leopold. No one but those with similar marks could see the symbols. Soul mates were often mistaken as the one true love of individuals, but that was an erroneous assumption. Legend told twin flames were one soul torn apart, forced to endure numerous reincarnations until they found one another. Oftentimes they rarely met in a lifetime. When they did, the chemistry was explosive. Humans that found their twin flames created great works together. When a paranormal discovered their flame, it wasn't just magical and cosmic, but prophetic, evidence the world geared up for a big change.

"Fuck me, I have it too," Leopold said from across the room.

"Ditto," Trench agreed.

"Told you she's ours," Sin gloated.

She wouldn't understand their language because no one on her planet had ever heard of it. Even if she could understand them, she most likely had no knowledge of a twin flame union. And knowing Sinner, he wouldn't have taken the time to explain. It was also apparent she hadn't come willingly.

Sinner lowered his head to place his lips a fraction from her ear and spoke in English for her benefit. "Be still."

She shivered as if he touched her, which was a good sign. It meant she felt them the way they felt her.

Sinner removed her gag before he released her arms from their bindings. She lifted her hands up toward her face, but Trench stopped her from removing her blindfold by placing the tip of the blade against her temple.

The woman froze and bit her bottom lip, but she notched her chin in a show of defiance. No words were necessary for her to understand what he wanted. After a moment, she balled her hands into fists and lowered her arms.

Sinner stepped into her back, holding her still as he muttered against her ear. "We don't want the merchandise hurt."

Trench glared at him.

"Stop being an ass," he told Sinner in Atlantian.

The drive to touch and draw her near was strong, but she wasn't ready for cuddles. Instead Trench gave his favorite blade the privilege of first touch. He slid the razor sharp knife along the material until the blindfold gave way. She blinked against the brightness of the room until she adjusted to the light and focused on Trench.

He met her bright purple eyes, shocked by their color. Heat sucker punched him in the gut, slithered through his body and settled into his chest where his heart pounded like he'd been boxing. Trench contemplated the idea that he already loved her.

That is moronic bullshit.

Romantic fuckery that would leave him hurt. It'd taken him years to trust Leopold even though they were twin flames. Yeah, he loved both of his men now, but his mother had dropped him off in the rock mines when he six. That proved how loyal love was. Didn't matter, he still wanted to give his heart to Sophia in this instant though.

She swiped her tongue along her bottom lip. A glass of water would aid her parched mouth, but he made no effort to move from her space. Trench couldn't move. He was too enraptured by her beauty even without the enhancement of makeup. Then again her planet didn't believe in beautifying a woman. It went against their religion to adorn her. It also went against their religion to allow women a voice. If he remembered correctly, only prostitutes used enhancements. And only the pariahs of society voiced an opinion.

Trench smiled at the realization that he was already smitten. Despite her sheltered upbringing she still had spunk.

She gawked at him; her violet eyes contrasted with her pale blonde hair. He had always loved blondes, but he'd never met a real blonde before either. Was hers natural?

From behind him, Leopold's steps struck the metal floor as he drew closer. "You're wearing too many clothes," he said in enunciated English. "Care to get naked?"

"No." The sound of her voice compelled Trench's cock to swell. With her jaw tightening, she squared her shoulders and tossed a lethal glare at Leopold. Trench opened and closed his hands to resist grabbing her and kissing the hell out of her in his way of saying welcome home.

Her eyes widened when she looked at Leopold. He was a sight to behold, much different than any of their appearances. Trench was simply pleased she didn't go into a fit of vapors at the sight of Leopold.

Leopold clucked his tongue. "Didn't think so."

"I'm Trench." He clasped her hand and lifted it as he turned her arm over to gaze at her wrist.

The evidence that she was their twin flame hit him like a meteor and a wave of dizziness crashed over him. She was theirs to love and protect, the evidence on all of their wrists. Any doubt before was eradicated in an instant.

If she knew what she walked into, she'd be terrified. As individuals they could be a lot to accommodate with their demands. United… yeah, they hadn't found a woman yet that could tolerate the three of them at once.

"Leopold," Leopold identified himself as he stepped to Trench's right. "You're stunning, love. Would you like something to drink?"

Trench noticed she withheld her name. Being sandwiched between him and Sinner probably increased her stress. They were big and intimidating men, both abrasive from growing up in the rock mines. Few survived the quarries, so they'd been lucky.

Most people felt more comfortable around Leopold. It seemed a man raised with all the luxuries of life generated a different effect on people's personalities. And he put people at ease despite being the most dangerous of them all. Trench and Sinner took lives, while Leopold ruined them with his connections. Their way was more merciful than Leopold's version.

She licked her lips again. "Yes, please. That'd be delightful."

Trench couldn't wait to experience her tongue on his body. He also wanted to drag his all over hers.

Leopold held his hand out to her. "Come, love." She glanced at Trench as if seeking his permission or daring him to stop her. Leopold whispered to her, "Ignore the Neanderthals. You have the privilege of doing whatever you want now; no need to ask for consent."

He pulled her along behind him and Trench turned to watch them. To Sinner, he asked, "Does she know?"

"No." Sinner pressed a button on his wrist and shook his head while his appearance returned to his normal looks. "Not unless her ghost told her."

Trench arched his eyebrows. "She has a ghost?"

Sinner shrugged and threaded his fingers through his black hair. "She's been talking to someone named Fred."

Sinner explained what happened and how she'd changed when Fred 'supposedly' took control of her body. Trench took that information in while he focused on her with Leopold.

Trench agreed she wore too many clothes, as was the custom on her planet, but he also eagerly looked forward to removing those clothes from her body. She moved with grace and entitlement. No wonder she meshed well with Leopold. She hadn't grown up hard or poor but knew the riches of life. Trench vowed she'd never know the hardship life offered others.

"What's her name?" he asked Sinner. "Or did you stop and ask before you kidnapped her?"

"No need to ask. I already knew it. Sophia Thornrose. The woman I was paid to kill."

Leopold glanced over his shoulder at them, his forehead grooved, proof he heard their conversation.

Trench jerked his head about to peer at Sinner. "You're fucking with me?"

"Nope." Sinner rocked on his heels. "I came this close"—he indicated with his fingers pinched together—"to killing our twin flame. It was dark when I had the chance to off her, but the sting on my wrist kept me from killing her. I didn't see the mark until I got her on the spaceship and showed it to you two."

What stuck out to Trench was that their woman was in danger. "You think taking her off planet will satisfy the person who hired you?"

"Doubtful." Sinner tore his gaze off Sophia to look at Trench. "That means I have a killer to find."

FOUR

Leopold

Leopold led the stunning blonde to the liquor bar. Her hair was a mess. Partially up with fistfuls of it hanging about her shoulders. His guess, Sinner had had his fingers in it.

Lucky bastard.

He couldn't wait to see all of it down. Preferably spread out on the sheets while he fucked her. That'd come, but it'd take time. At the moment, if she had access to a gun or knife or just some basic fighting skills she'd most likely fuck them all up, starting with Sinner.

He glanced at his lovers, Sinner and Trench. He hadn't heard all of their conversation, but he'd caught enough. Someone wanted their twin flame dead. Ironically without the assassination job, they'd never have found her. They had no reason to visit this planet. Very little of Uriel's resources were used in their technologically advanced universe, so they couldn't even use this visit as a requisition job.

"What's your name?" he asked in English as he poured her a shot of dragon venom. She looked like she needed a stiff drink.

She shook her head. "Water please."

Leopold arched an eyebrow at her and diluted the dragon venom with water. He offered her the glass once more.

They stared at one another, a standoff of sorts. She made no move to accept the glass. Leopold refused to take no for an answer.

He nodded at the glass he held toward her. "Love—"

"Don't call me that." She tilted her head at a pretentious angle but given her petite height he found it cute more than condescending. "I'm *not* your love."

"I'm not attempting to be a hard ass." He'd leave the assholery to Sinner and Trench. They excelled at it and he was better at wooing women than either of them. "You're in a difficult situation not of your choosing. Work with me and I'll make the transition easier."

She placed her sapphire velveted arm on the wet bar—the fabric had to be heavy—and leaned toward him. "Work with me and grant me my freedom."

Leopold loved her spirit.

He placed the goblet on the bar in front of her. "This," he indicated the twin flame mark on her wrist, "indicates you *are* free."

She frowned when she peered at her skin. "Where'd that come from?"

His new twin flame dipped her finger in the watered down dragon venom and scrubbed at the spots. It didn't fade or erase the three identical designs each resting above the other in a vertical line.

"I have three of them. One for Trench, Sinner, and now you." He placed his arm on the table top next to hers and folded back his sleeve to display his identical symbols. "These tell me you belong to us."

"I belong to no one," she said, but the look in her eyes hinted at something else.

"Does it make you feel better to know we belong to you as well?" he asked noting Sinner and Trench drew closer so they could hear the conversation.

"I don't want to own men. I don't agree with slavery."

Leopold chuckled. "We're not your slaves. On your planet, you'd call us husbands."

"Hmm..." She tapped her chin with a finger. "What would I do with three husbands? One of you could cook, the other clean, and the last one fan me and feed me grapes."

Fucking adorable. She teased them.

Leopold smiled. "Why aren't you scandalized?"

She looked to his right as if listening to someone or maybe she was gathering her thoughts. He was kind of impressed she wasn't throwing her goblet at his head. Giving her upbringing on her backward world, the twin flame information was a lot to process.

"I am, can't you tell?" she said deadpan.

They stared at one another. Why'd he get the feeling she knew more than she let on?

"How does this tell you anything?" She scrubbed at the symbols on her wrist once more. "Where'd it come from? Why do we have it? Do they have it too?" She glanced over her shoulder to indicate Sinner and Trench.

Trench showed off by pulling his shirt over his head and dropping it on the floor. Well-muscled, Trench enjoyed working out in the gym, boxing, and was disciplined in dozens of different fighting styles. Leopold went with a subtler firepower like poison or guns, or if he really wanted to watch someone swing in the wind, he'd use the League of Ambassadors to ruin their lives. Those ways were more effective than Trench's old-fashioned violence.

Sophia's interest surfaced as fast as Trench removed his shirt. She stepped to him and gawked at his tattoos. "The paint on your skin is exquisite."

"They're what we call tattoos," Trench said, his voice gruff. "It's ink put beneath the skin. Won't wash off. Feel."

Trench held his arm toward her, and she moved closer to him. With one hand she cradled his forearm and with the other, she trailed her fingertips over his ink. Leopold had never been so jealous of another man in all his life.

"I have them too." Sinner practically ripped his shirt off.

Leopold rolled his eyes.

When she peered at Sinner her eyes widened. "Your face changed, but your voice is the same."

"I use a vanity chip to alter my appearance." He held his arm out toward her like Trench had.

She obliged and touched him, her thumb stroking along the twin flame markings. "I don't understand these. How'd I get a tattoo?"

"Tell me your name and I'll answer your questions." Leopold made the offer.

She huffed. "Sophia Thornrose."

"It's a pleasure meeting you, Sophia." Leopold sipped the dragon venom in his glass. "These marks are called twin flame marks." Once again she revealed zero emotion, as if none of this surprised her. "What are you hiding, Sophia?"

FIVE

Sophia

"Nothing." Sophia held Leopold's golden eyes as Trench explained the story about twin flames and cosmic destiny. She'd heard it all before thanks to Fred. Nodding, she inhaled and held her breath, letting the air burn her lungs before she released it. "Would you prefer hysterics instead?"

Fred ignored her and plundered the wet bar.

"You realize you're part of a foursome, right?" Leopold did not look away, so she felt obliged to maintain his stare. Not that she had a hard time staring at him.

Even though he boasted orange and light, silvery blue skin, golden eyes, and blonde hair, she found him attractive. Handsome enough she wanted to cross her legs for fear her heat would divulge her arousal by dripping down her thighs.

"Only brothels provide those types of services on Uriel," Trench said.

SOPHIA'S CONNECTION

She widened her eyes as if shocked by the foursome. Leopold narrowed his like he was the big bad wolf in the story that ate everyone, and he didn't believe her shock. She should've known she couldn't fool him, but a gut feeling suggested he'd keep her secret.

As a child, she'd fantasized about being the bad ass that defeated the wolf. Staring into the eyes of the real wolf, she'd let him eat her first.

She let a little smile tug one corner of her mouth. The gleam that brightened Leopold's gold eyes came in an instant.

She turned to face Trench. He was a dark-skinned giant. He looked at her like he'd eat her too. That stare of his made her stomach flutter. It was odd because no man had ever created this effect in her, and never *three* men. She'd had lovers, but not more than one man at a time. The logistics of sleeping with three at once should terrify her, but her blood heated instead.

Trench wasn't the type of man she'd normally find attractive because of his obvious brooding dominance. There was something about his rugged appearance, with his pigtail braids, and heavy beard that appealed to her though. His silver eyes held creases at the corners and something about the way he observed her said he'd seen more horror than any man should have to tolerate in a lifetime.

Sinner was no different. His vibe was lethal, his stare one that said no one screwed with him and lived, and while he displayed a hard edge similar to Trench's, Sinner's was more subtle.

How he pulled off a hard edge with his new stunning appearance, she couldn't imagine, because all she wanted to do was taste him like she would chocolate. His abs were as tight as Trench's and they both reeked of power. His green eyes stared at her much the same was as Trench's golden ones did, both with too much dark cynicism for their young years.

Leopold made her feel comfortable, but she sensed the danger in him as well. It was a restrained vibe and he hid it well beneath his cultivated veneer.

Sophia glanced between the three of them. She'd never felt truly safe in her life, until now. She looked at Fred who stood next to Leopold. "What's your reaction to this nonsense?"

Fred shrugged and she wanted to beat him over the head with a cast iron skillet.

Leopold glanced at the other guys. "I already told you what I *know*."

"Apologies." Normally she didn't directly speak to Fred in front of others, but Sinner already knew about Fred and if her future was to work with these three they had to know what they were getting into. "I'm speaking to Fred, not you."

"Um... who's Fred?" Leopold turned to face the direction she peered.

"My spirit guide." She held Leopold gaze, waiting for him to laugh at her declaration or declare her immediate death.

"Hell, yeah." Leopold grinned, his tone one of excitement.

"We not only have a beautiful woman, but a powerful one too," Trench drawled.

Leopold pointed to his right. "Is your Fred standing here?"

Sophia nodded, blinking at them in confusion. Sinner hadn't believed her, but Trench and Leopold seemed excited by her news.

"What does your Fred say?" Trench asked, stepping near Leopold to snag a glass and spirits.

"Fred says," her spirit guide dipped his finger in her glass and licked his finger, "this liquor is fantastic."

"He likes the liquor you poured me." Sophia walked to the sofa, perched on the edge like a lady should, slanted her legs and crossed her ankles. She removed her hairpins since long strands hung around her face. Thanks to Sinner her two-hour updo was in shambles.

"Is that real?" Trench came to her and sat on the sofa next to her.

"Of course, Fred's real, but I don't expect any of you to believe me." Only her clients were believers. If her father wasn't first cousins with the King, she probably would've already been hung for crimes against the Church.

"Not that." Trench waved his hand. "I believe you about Fred. Hi, dude, but don't interfere in my shit." Trench glanced about with an elevated eyebrow as if laying down the law to Fred.

Leopold carried two glasses toward her. "We all believe that."

She glanced at Sinner and he nodded. "You didn't believe me before you abducted me. Why now?"

Sinner shrugged. "I'm a half believer, but that they believe you is good enough for me."

Trench clarified. "Your hair. Is it real?"

"Oh." She twisted the long strands and wound them to form a bun at the back of her head. "Yes, I don't wear wigs. They are dreadful contraptions made to torment humanity."

"Leave it down," Sinner said in a gruff voice.

"Please." Leopold gave Sinner a stern glance as he took the seat across from her and placed her goblet on the table between them.

"Yes, it's beautiful." Trench lifted his hand and paused before he touched her hair. "May I?"

Sophia licked her lips. In her world only a husband touched a woman's hair. It was an intimate request.

The devil that caused so much trouble in her life and kidnapped her said, "Let him. He let you touch him."

She gulped, released her hair, and dragged her fingers through the strands to remove any tangles. It felt like he moved in slow motion as Trench reached to stroke her hair.

Trench leaned in to skim the ends through his fingertips. "So soft." He dragged his fingers through the mass, and she shivered at his closeness. His olive complexion accentuated his dark features and silver eyes. But it was his lips that captured her attention. Wide, sensual, and she craved to know how they'd feel on hers.

SOPHIA'S CONNECTION

Sophia looked up at him. She held her breath for a moment but released it as she gazed into his beautiful eyes. They were wide and his mouth had parted, a sigh slipping past his lips as if in rapture.

"I'm awed someone like you would be gifted to us." Trench rubbed her hair against his lips.

She smiled, awed in return that someone as dangerous as him would look at her with such reverence. "I'm no saint, Trench."

"You're a virgin." Sinner smirked and sat on the arm of the sofa next to her.

Uncomfortable with that assumption, she shifted in her seat.

"So?" She focused on Sinner, worried he'd be disappointed when he discovered the truth. His black hair shined in the lighting. The scruff on his jaw gave him a pirate vibe and in a way he was pirate-ish. He'd abducted her to his ship. In her world men were clean shaven, so their beards intrigued her and crafted a hardened vibe that wasn't altogether real.

Leopold explained, "Where we're from, no one is a virgin anymore." He sipped his liquor and looked at her over the rim. Sophia elevated her eyebrows at him, and he said, "Some parents remove their daughter's hymen at birth. Other species aren't born with one."

Desire churned in her belly and her hands shook at the thought of taking on three men. Placing her hands in her lap, she glanced between them.

"How does it work? The three of us?" She sighed and slumped against the cushions; thankful her father wasn't there to criticize her posture. "Together at once. Is it even possible?"

Leopold smirked and she for once got the feeling he believed her question was genuine. How could he read her lies so easily.

Fred laughed, startling her from the conversation with her men. "You wouldn't believe the stuff they have in this cabinet." His head peeked up from behind the wet bar. "They're not only stocked here, but also in their pants."

"Don't be crass, Fred," she shot back, sitting up straight once again.

"Why not. I can tell you're worried about their size and how you'll take them all at once." He stood from behind the bar. "For the record, it's doable. Relax and stop second guessing everything."

"It's what I do," she shot back.

"What'd Fred say?" Leopold asked as he stared at her wearing a mini-frown. "What is it that you do?"

She felt the flush hit her cheeks.

Leopold grinned and teased, "I'm guessing it's nothing a *lady* should repeat."

"That's the thing, beautiful." Sinner coiled a lock of her hair around his finger, drawing her attention to him. "In our world you don't have to be a lady."

"Yup," Trench agreed. "You can reinvent yourself without receiving censure from anyone."

Leopold sat forward and placed his elbows on his knees. His glass dangled from his fingers. "You're free to be out of the closet." She looked at his smirking mouth and resisted the compulsion to press hers to his. "Be your wicked, dirty self."

"There's a lot you don't know about our world," Sinner muttered.

"A lot you'll loathe," Trench agreed.

She inclined her head at her kidnapper. "Like how I loathe that you're an assassin, Sinner?"

"Yeah." He shrugged. "You'll likely loathe other things worse, but my job as an assassin saved your life." Sinner slid a thumb along her jaw. "Don't forget that. Fate brought us together for that purpose. Fate also made the four of us for one another."

"I wish I'd found my twin flame in my life." Fred approached them. "You don't realize how lucky you are."

She rubbed her temples. "It's so much to take in."

Eager to get to her new life, she hated the game she played with them, but worried they'd question too much if she gave in too quickly.

Leopold pushed her glass closer to her. "Drink this and then I'll take you to your room. You can bathe and put on some clean clothes. Talk to your spirit. We'll dine together in a few hours and answer any questions you have."

She stared at the goblet. "Ladies don't drink liquor."

Trench plucked her glass off the table and offered it to her. "That's your decision now. No judgment from us if you drink it, but it will help you relax."

Sophia took the glass from his hand and sipped at the contents. "Mmm... this is delicious."

All of her men smiled at her.

Her men. Life is kind.

SIX

Leopold

Leopold guided her to their bedroom. She allowed his touch on her lower back as he navigated her through the ship.

He never slept apart from his twin flames unless one was off planet. While he could lead her to separate quarters, after that bullshit she pulled he suspected she knew more than she let on. He also suspected she wanted them every bit as much as they wanted her.

His bullshit meter had been tapdancing on his spine. She'd fooled Trench and Sinner with her innocent routine, but not him.

Ragaran's were truth-seekers and as a species could discern lies. They held no preconceived notions about a person's life and accepted all races and lifestyles.

"Is your spirit friend with us?"

"He's always with me."

"Even when you fuck?"

She looked up at him, her mouth dropping in surprise.

"Don't pretend innocence with me, Sophia." He added pressure to the right side of her hip, and she turned as he wanted. That she followed his direction without words pleased him. "I don't understand the game you're playing, but you're not a virgin."

She halted in the hallway and leaned against the wall. "You don't know that."

Leopold chuckled. He could explain how his kind could discern the truth but elected to hide that while she continued to play games. "No, not until I get you beneath me and my dick inside you."

Sophia bit her bottom lip and turned her head aside. He caught the way her breasts hitched thanks to her sudden breath.

Leopold leaned toward her and placed his forearm on the wall next to her head. He lifted a hand and trailed his fingers along her exposed collarbone. "Does that idea excite you, love?"

"Can I be frank with you without judgment from you?"

The vulnerability in her eyes had him lowering his hand. "Of course. The same can be applied to Trench and Sinner."

"You think I was playing games and maybe I am, but you boys were treating me like a brainless twit." She lifted her chin in a defiant manner but held his gaze. The truth evident in her purple eyes. "You wanted to get me drunk, while

Trench and Sinner wanted to play pet the fragile doll."

His first thought was to argue over being described as a boy. His second was surprise. She'd caught onto their protective instinct and resisted their testosterone drive. Their intention wasn't to suppress her, but he could see how she would've felt smothered.

But petting the fragile doll? Really? For fuck's sake that came off as snooty. "You have a problem with them being into you? Wanting to protect you?"

"No. I have a problem with being worshipped. Trench said as much, that he didn't deserve me. None of you know what I've done or if *I* deserve *you*."

He laughed. "Have you killed anyone?" When she shook her head, he went on. "Have you ruined a life?"

"Not that I know of." She frowned at him.

"Yeah, you're a terrible person, Sophia."

"I'm a freak because I was born with the ability to see dead people and I have a ghost stalker."

"We're all freaks in some way. Look at me. Your people would call me a freak and I look like you except for the coloration of my skin."

"I like your skin." She touched his arm near her head. "It's softer than mine too."

"It's thicker than yours and can repel bullets."

"Superhero," she teased with a lift to the corners of her lips.

He smiled and scratched at his jaw while gazing at her. "So... you're not fragile, huh?"

"No."

"You think you can handle us?"

"I was designed for you three with that in mind, right? At least that's what you boys tell me."

"Do I look like a *boy*, love?"

Sophia shivered and licked her lips, the move quickening his blood. Leopold stepped into her personal space, a slow move so he wouldn't alarm her. She surprised him when she placed her palm on the center of his chest, as if to halt his approach, but instead she slid her hand up and around his neck, tugging him forward.

"Do *you* think I can handle all of you?"

He gulped and followed her lead, following her unspoken tug until his body aligned against hers. Too much fabric separated them, but the prudishness of the material coupled with her forthcoming manner, excited him.

"Let's find out," he said as he used his fingers to haul her skirt up enough he could dip his hand beneath the cloth.

Sophia leaned her head against the wall and stared at his face. Leopold cupped the side of her thigh and drew the material upward to her waist. He used his knee to widen her legs as he slid his hand over her belly and downward to her core. Her frilly undergarments got in the way, so he ripped the delicate lace.

Her breath hitched, drawing his gaze to the swell of her cleavage, satisfied his savagery increased her arousal. As his fingers found her hot and wet, he bent his head and licked where her tits pressed together.

A tiny gasp exited her lungs as she fisted his hair. Leopold lifted his head and held her eyes as he tested her by pushing a finger into her. As her eyes darkened to a dark purple, she bit her bottom lip and wrapped her leg around his hip, an open invitation to play with her intimately.

"Love, I think you're going to shock Trench and Sinner." He kissed her and she opened to him. Their tongues tangled to a seductive dance while he added another finger and thrust them into her.

Her other hand held onto his shoulder as her hips rocked into his slid in. She whimpered into his mouth on the exit of his fingers. He circled her swollen clit with his thumb, and she used her hold on his head to jerk his head back.

"Go-gonna c-come." Mouth parted, she panted as she held his eyes.

She knew! She fucking *knew* he'd want to watch her come.

Fascinated by her wanton behavior after exhibiting innocence in their initial meeting, he fucked her harder with his fingers. Sophia gifted him with this private moment.

With a soft cry, she climaxed, her channel clenching around his penetration while he saw her through to the last of her pleasure. Cheeks flushed, she went lax against the wall and towed him to her for a soft kiss.

"Will you tell them?" she murmured against his mouth.

"Don't know." He knew she asked if he'd tell Trench and Sinner about this moment. In all honesty, he couldn't say what he'd tell them, if anything. But he also didn't want them to think he withheld secrets from them either. The four of them were a team, a partnership, all of them in a relationship. They'd share her and there was no room for jealousy.

He withdrew his fingers from her wet pussy. She whimpered at his withdrawal, but when he pushed them against her mouth they licked her essence off together. Dirty women were their cup of tea.

SEVEN

Sinner

Sin and Trench sipped dragon venom, neither speaking while Leopold showed Sophia to their bedroom. Whoever wanted her dead had access to the intergalactic communication system, which meant her would-be killer wasn't a native of Uriel.

Why target Sophia? No one knew of his twin flame connection with Trench or Leopold. To his knowledge no one could deduce a twin flame connection, except for those involved. That he discovered another twin was nothing more than blind chance.

The door slid open and Leopold entered the room. "I hope you have a means of keeping her safe, Sinner."

Sinner ran his fingers through his hair and leaned into the sofa cushions. "I want her chipped with a vanity chip as soon as possible. Nanites installed."

Only the three of them would have access to her true beauty. None could be trusted with her exact looks or they'd risk her safety. And the nanites would heal her on the off chance someone got lucky enough to get to her.

"No one but us should ever know her true identity or appearance." Trench downed his liquor. "We should change her name just in case."

Leopold nodded and strode to the bar. "If we play this right, whoever hired you to kill her won't know she remains alive."

Sinner pushed to his feet and set his glass on the wet bar for Leopold to refill. He crossed to a wall, waved his hand in front of it and the panels slid open to reveal space. Stars zipped past as their ship, Raging Waters, moved through solar systems in seconds.

He'd been friends with Trench since they were boys working in the rock mine on the planet Mira where all criminals or indebted individuals were sent to pay for their crimes or bills. Sinner had been born in the quarry to a mother who'd made a living as a whore to survive. Trench moved to the quarry at the age of six when his mother abandoned him there.

At their first meeting the twin flame mark had appeared on their arms. Trench had heard of the lore, but Sinner had been ignorant. From that moment on, they'd become fast friends, thicker than thieves, always having one another's back. Sinner couldn't count the number of times they'd saved one another's life.

The rock mine had been back breaking work but toughened them and made them resilient. Thanks to the physical work, they'd grown strong enough to escape as teenagers. For a time, they'd worked as assassins and space pirates, stealing ships, cargo, and even selling people into slavery.

That's when they'd met Leopold. As the son of an intergalactic senator, Trench and Sinner had known the identity of the individual on the ship when they boarded it and took control. They'd planned to ransom Leopold back to his parents for a hefty profit. Instead they'd found their unexpected third twin-flame.

"What's on your mind, Sinner?" Leopold interrupted his thoughts as he approached Sinner and offered him a refilled goblet.

Sinner took the glass. "Did anyone know twin flames could come in foursomes?"

"I've heard rumors." Trench shrugged and settled into his seat more comfortably.

"Can we expect a fifth to join us? Or a sixth?" Sinner downed his liquor while telling himself to slow the fuck down before he got drunk. Sophia needed him level-headed and at his best, not inebriated. "It's going to get crowded in bed if we start adding more."

Leopold frowned. "Are you disappointed fate's given her to us?"

"Fuck no," Sinner snarled. "I'm pissed off someone wants her dead and thankful I was the one hired, or we'd never have found her. She'd have been lost to us forever."

Trench released a relieved sounding breath. "We move forward like she's the last one, but if we find more, then we consider ourselves blessed."

Sinner nodded and peered at his fisted hand. There on his left wrist was what looked like a birthmark, a faint darkening of his skin in the odd, but familiar twin flame shape. Strange how that one simple thing changed their entire world.

Sinner barely knew Sophia, but he'd fight to the death to keep her safe. He would do *anything* to give her a world of power and protection. Fuck, hadn't the three of them done the same for one another. Fifteen years had passed since finding Leopold. In that time, Sinner had won a planet in a card game and turned it into a paradise where all desires, dark and clean, could be fulfilled. No sin went unfulfilled on Atlantis. Even the worst crimes like murder, rape, and pedophilia were satisfied on their planet. They weren't good men and they had built their lives around debauchery.

What would Sophia think of that?

"I finger fucked her before I put her in our bedroom," Leopold said into the lingering silence. "She's not the innocent either of you believe her to be."

"Fuck me." Sinner gaped at Leopold, torn between jealousy and admiration.

Trench leapt to his feet and strode toward them demanding, "What'd she taste like? Feel like? *Sound like* when she came?"

Sinner chuckled. "Thank fuck. I was worried we'd have to move slowly with her."

EIGHT

Sophia

Life had been dull. Sophia Thornrose could count the passage of years by the dances and tea parties she attended. A snooze fest. There had to be more to life. She'd lamented her boredom to Fred often.

From her bedroom window on her planet, she'd spent hours watching the ships chug in and out of the harbor. She fancied their quest for adventures on the high seas. Some would be artifact collectors and treasure hunters. Sometimes they'd battle Wendigos on the African peninsula—not that the average person believed in Wendigos, but these were *her* fantasies. As the adventurers ran for their lives, shooting silver bullets over their shoulders, they'd barely make it to their ship in time. But even through the desperate race across rocky terrain, they would've succeeded in acquiring the beetle from King Tut's sarcophagus. Any man that found that would be a hero since it was reputed to have magical properties. At least that's what Fred claimed.

Other times her drama-inspired battles involved space-pirates in deep space. Those fantasies were thanks to Fred's ability to detail tall tales of otherworldly planets and different races.

She'd craved meeting different races. Wanted to see firsthand what other people looked like. She hadn't anticipated discovering one of her lovers would have satiny soft blue and orange skin either. Neither had she suspected he'd be bold enough to get her off in the hallway of an actual spaceship.

Although her romantic fantasies differed from reality, she had no complaints. In her daydreams, the hero fell madly in love with her and gave up all his criminal enterprises for her.

I don't want that.

Just because she knew little about the three men that were her life-mates, asking them to change now would constitute an unforgiveable sin in her mind. They should be themselves as much as she craved acceptance for who she was.

Thanks to Sinner she was headed straight for another planet with three dark, controlling men, one of which was an assassin. But that killer had saved her life.

She'd never even seen the New World her father, the Duke of Redesdale, had spoken of. He'd visited the modern territory and been appalled by the freedoms they gave women.

I'll take that freedom, thank you, and a slice of yum to go with it. Three yums to be precise.

At the thought of Trench, Sinner, and Leopold, she fanned herself. Leopold gave her a taste of what was to come as their woman, and she was eager to test them out.

She blinked at the stars that sped past her at an alarming rate and wondered if she'd ever see her father again?

How long would he grieve before he stopped looking for her?

Sophia swallowed past the tight knot in her throat. Despite his stoicism, she loved her father.

"Will I like their home planet, Fred?"

"I suspect Atlantis comes with a learning curve, but you'll acclimate easier than another of your kinship." Fred stood in the middle of the bed, part of his body disappearing into the furniture. "This mattress is huge. They must all sleep on it together."

They all bore the same mark in the same spot on their wrists. She hadn't considered that the three men might also share an intimate relationship with one another until now. Stomach fluttering at the thought, her blood heated again. She rubbed her arms, worried at this rate she'd stay in a constant state of arousal.

"Atlantis will be your safe haven." Rose, the deceased mother of Sinner Prometheus, smiled. She'd joined them thirty minutes ago, surprising Sophia with her appearance. "You'll love Atlantis," Rose went on. "It's a pirates' metropolis. All their desires can be met there, but they fear my boy and his husbands."

"Why?" Sophia asked. Yeah, Sinner held that dangerous vibe, but she felt no fear from him. She was interested in them and how they'd gotten to where they are now.

"He doesn't tolerate bullshit," Rose muttered with a grin stretching her pale cheeks. Dark haired like Sinner, she was lighter skinned with dark blue eyes. Young, maybe twenty when she died. Her language testified to her lower class upbringing, but what did money and status matter when none of them escaped death?

"Atlantis is located next door to a black hole that can eat a spacecraft if Sinner decides to toss them inside it." Rose grinned again; her eyes glowing as she bounced about on her feet. "I like it when Sinner tosses bad people into the black hole." She pressed two fingers to her lips to stop her giggle. "It's fun watching them beg for mercy when they showed none before their punishment."

Fred scowled at Rose. "What type of crimes are black hole punishable?"

Rose rubbed at her arms, a malicious smile curling the corners of her mouth. "Pissing off my son."

Sophia frequently endured dishonorable gentlemen but she had a gut feeling her twin flames would demonstrate more honor. They would require genuine, unthinkable crimes before the black hole came into play.

"Rose is batshit crazy." Fred shook his head at her.

Sinner's mother giggled like a schoolgirl.

Sophia rolled her eyes. Just what she need, a senseless spirit tagging along. Before she could say more, the door swished open, and she turned away from the window to see who'd entered.

Trench and Leopold walked into their bedroom. Sophia couldn't help but glance at the bed. Their presence brought to mind the sweet touch of Leopold and his kisses. More of that wonderfulness would occur on that bed.

Trench approached her with a mocking smile tilting the corners of his sexy mouth. He wore black leather pants and a pull over vest-like shirt in the same color, with black, lace-up boots. Leopold wore similar attire, but a loose top billowed over his arms while the vest pressed the fabric to his chest. Strange straps held foot-wear to the soles of his feet.

Trench stopped in front of her, his boots touching her toes. "Did you enjoy the orgasm Leopold gave you?"

Surprised Leopold confessed their actions, she sent him a sharp glance.

"We don't have secrets," Leopold admitted.

"Yes." She met Trench's gaze dead-on. "You jealous?"

"No. Yes." He laughed. "You're ours, you don't belong to just one of us, so you're welcome to try out any of us any time you want."

She leaned toward him. "Is that an offer, Trench?"

"Not yet."

Stomach clenching, she looked at her hands and picked at her nails. That she'd read him wrong, dismayed her. Geez… she would've never guessed navigating relationships to be this uncertain.

"Don't pout." Trench's hand slipped to the back of her neck.

"I'm not." She looked up at him as he tugged her closer and loomed over her. His strong presence represented power and how easy he could dominate her. That ignited a burn in her belly. "I'm unsure how to move forward with any of you. With Leopold it felt natural to make out with him."

"Can't wait to do it again with you, love." When she glanced at Leopold he winked at her.

Sophia smiled at him, some of her doubt leaving her in a rush.

"Leopold has his way. I have mine." Trench lifted his other hand and curled his finger beneath her chin, tipping her head back. "I want you to understand who and what I am, the bastard I am, the monster inside me, before you 'make out' with me. Make out." He chuckled and shook his head. "That sounds like we're on a prom date."

"I don't know what that is," she confessed.

He kissed her nose. "Doesn't matter."

A sudden lightness lifted her mood and she leaned into him. Sophia wrapped her arms around his waist, his solid chest an inadequate buffer against her tight nipples.

Trench ran his fingers through her hair as he pressed his lips against hers. She went onto her tiptoes to get a better taste of him.

"Look at me," he said against her lips.

Her eyes fluttered open to find him watching her. Both of his hands in her hair fisted on either side of her head, and he kissed the hell out of her. Taking and dominating, his tongue driving in to claim hers and force a sensual dance.

Sophia moaned into him, her eyes slipping closed again to concentrate on his tongue against hers. She felt his hands shift and move down her back. Shivering at his touch, she craved more, his flesh on hers, his cock driving into her. Leopold had primed her, and she craved more.

Her dress loosened and she could breathe easier.

Trench broke away from the kiss and she tried to follow his mouth, but he took a few steps backward. "You suck cock as good as you kiss?"

She smiled at the question and touched her mouth with her fingers. "No. That's not a thing on Uriel."

"It's a thing, love." Leopold smirked. "Even on Uriel."

Trench grinned. "I promise you it's a thing." He pointed at Leopold. "Sinner is preparing dinner and we came to collect you. Leopold brought you attire from our planet."

At his name, Leopold placed a small purple piece of fabric on the bed.

"Where's the rest of it?" There wasn't nearly enough fabric there to call it clothing. "That thing wouldn't cover one-inch of skin."

"Your current dress is outdated." Leopold came up behind her and kissed her nape. "You'll draw the wrong type of attention wearing it and once we reach Atlantis, we need you to be incognito while in the presence of others."

Trench cleared his throat. "We thought you'd prefer to wear the new outfit around us before we dock in Atlantis tomorrow."

"Yep." Leopold nipped at her neck and she gasped at the fire it elicited between her thighs. "To help you feel more comfortable in the presence of others."

Sophia gawked at the one-by-one inch square of purple cloth. "You're teasing me?"

"No." Leopold curled his fingers around the fabric at the top of her arms and tugged the garment down.

She leaned her head back against his shoulder and met his eyes. Leopold kissed her temple before drawing her dress down to her feet. He kissed one of her butt cheeks and she reached back to grab his blond hair.

Trench's gaze slid along her frilly underthings. "You undergarments are another layer of clothes."

She touched her pussy with her other hand and tugged at the frayed material. "Leopold tore them."

"Fuck." Trench's fingers combed his beard. "If Sinner was present I'd eat your pussy."

She felt her eyes widen. The visual of his head between her legs sparked interest. With saliva wetting her tongue she asked, "That's a thing?"

Trench laughed and Leopold chuckled against her lower back.

"Oh, yeah, love." Through her clothes, Leopold nipped her butt, a slight sting that brought a fast pulse. "That's damn sure a thing. We'll be fighting over who teaches you that first."

"You made her come first *without* me and Sinner." Trench stared at Leopold over her shoulder. "You do *not* get to eat her pussy first."

"He thinks he's the boss of everyone." Leopold said against neck, indicating he'd stood.

Trench lifted his eyebrows. "You deny I'm the boss of you in the bedroom?"

She felt Leopold's lips curl against her skin.

"So, you *are* intimate with each other." The idea of these three men touching one another caused a surge of heat to throb against her intimate lips, drawing out a physical ached for the familiarity they spoke of.

Trench's brooding stare shifted into amusement. "Undress or I can do it for you."

"Have at it." She lifted both arms up to reach back and clutch Leopold's head.

Trench pulled his knife from its holster at his hip and dragged it along a few areas of her underwear. Her undies caressed her skin as it fell away from her body, leaving her exposed to their gazes, yet she felt sensual and desired without any uncertainty.

"Damn." Trench stared at her breasts before lowering his gaze to the rest of her body.

Leopold stepped away from her hold to assess her. He whistled.

Making a slow turn for them to view all of her, she sent them what she hoped was a flirty smile. "Do I pass inspection?"

"Fuck yeah," Leopold's voice went rough.

"Never doubt it." Trench picked up the purple square from the bed and handed it to her. "It smart adjusts."

"Meaning?"

Leopold grasped her hand and clasped a bracelet onto her wrist. "It's better if we show you. Place the fabric here." He took the material from her grasp and placed it on her forearm. "Push this button and you're set."

Trench nodded. "The diem—"

"That's the material-slash-dress on your arm," Leopold clarified.

"Yeah. Don't be surprised when it moves to cover your body."

"Okay." Sophia pressed the button Leopold indicated. The 'diem' came to life and slid over her body, covering her in a pantsuit. She looked down at her frame and laughed. The technology was wonderful, even if it fit her like a layer of purple skin.

"I knew the cat suit would look fantastic on her." Leopold gave her a chaste kiss, but his gaze spoke of sexual corruption. "You're beautiful."

"Sexy." Trench's eyes gleamed at her as his contemplation prowled over her.

"*Rawr*," she teased with a growl.

NINE

Trench

The filmy fabric hid everything of importance but also showed off her delectable curves. She came in somewhere around five-five, with the top of her head coming to Trench's chin. Leopold stood at six foot, Sinner at six-two, and Trench at six-eight. She looked tiny against all of them, but he bet she could hold her own.

She already holds her own against us three.

He preferred her naked, but the catsuit served as the closest substitute. He couldn't wait for Sinner to see her.

Trench laced his fingers with her right hand and Leopold took her left. Together they walked along the hallway toward the kitchen.

"I can't wait to show you how good my tongue will feel against your nipples and pussy." Trench licked his lips. He couldn't fucking wait.

She turned her head to look up at him. "Will I like it?"

"I will." He chuckled.

"Trench is a master at oral sex," Leopold confirmed. "You'll love it so much you'll beg for his tongue on your pussy."

"I enjoy exhausting my lovers with pleasure before shoving my dick inside them." At Trench's graphic words, her breath hitched, and her eyes dilated.

Sophia licked her lips and Trench took that as a sign of interest.

"I can attest to that." Leopold sighed. "Guess I'm spoiled because I've always enjoyed being the center of his and Sinner's attention."

"You still will be," Trench shifted his gaze to Leopold. "Nothing changes except we have someone else at the center with you."

"Whew." Sophia fanned herself. "When can we get started on those diabolical promises."

Trench chuckled.

"After dinner?" Hope elevated Leopold's voice.

"My preference is that Sophia *is* dinner," Sinner said from the kitchen doorway. "But I have questions and I know she does too." He looked at Trench. "What took so fucking long?"

"I saw her naked, Sinner." Trench elevated his eyebrows. "Thank me for not fucking her without you."

"You fucker. Both of you are fuckers." Sinner held his hand out toward Sophia. "You look beautiful."

"Better naked," Leopold replied.

"She will look even better with my dick inside her," Trench contradicted.

She sent them a cheeky grin before releasing their hands and grabbing Sinner's. "I wouldn't object to any of you getting naked."

"Can I kiss you?" Sinner snuggled her against his muscled frame.

Trench resisted joining them, even though he wanted to sandwich her between them.

"Do you normally ask?" She ran her fingertips over Sinner's stubbly jaw.

"No." Sinner nipped at her fingertips.

She smiled at him.

That smile was all Sinner needed to take the kiss from her. Their mouths came together, and Sophia melted against him. The kiss deepened and she moaned into his mouth.

Watching her with Sinner was hotter than hellfire. Trench adjusted his cock in his leather pants, but the new angle provided no comfort.

Sophia's stomach growled and she giggled against Sinner's mouth.

"Let's feed our woman," Trench demanded.

Sinner smiled at her. The look in his lover's eyes was softer than Trench had ever seen his partner look at a person. Trench predicted she'd change the dynamics of their family more than any of them could've expected.

TEN

Leopold

Leopold grasped Sophia's hand and guided her to a chair. "We have a short trip before we reach Atlantis. I recommend we use this time to our advantage because life will change once we reach home."

"How?" Sophia went willingly with Leopold.

He pulled out a chair for her and waited for her to sit. "Everyone will want a peek at the woman who caught our attention."

Sinner set a plate in front of her and she peered at the offering. "I would like to have you modified when we arrive in Atlantis."

That request drew her attention away from the food. Frowning at Sinner, she placed her hands in her lap and her spine went straight. "Modified how? Why?"

Her posture felt tight to Leopold, and he sensed she entered a defensive mode. Being rejected by society would keep a person on guard. "It's not what you think, love."

"I guess we'll see." She leaned into her chair, holding Sinner's gaze. "Explain."

Sinner smiled. "Normally I'd say something about people wrongly assuming they can boss me around, but it's sexy coming from you."

Sophia didn't break a smile.

"We love you just how you are." Trench sat next to Sinner across the table from Leopold and Sophia.

"The modification is to protect you." Sinner poured her a glass of leviathan wine. "We'll always be honest with you, Sophia. Never doubt that you're important to us, that we love you the way you are."

"It's too soon to toss around the L word," she said, her posture unbreaking.

"No, but I already like you." Sinner set the wine bottle aside. "When you're with us, we'll want you just like you are."

"Except naked. I always prefer naked."

"Trench, you're hung up on that." Leopold winked at his husband before sliding his gaze to Sophia. "But for the record, I always prefer naked too."

An amused twitch ghosted her lips. "I expect the same from you guys. If I'm naked, you're naked."

"That'll be my pleasure." Trench toasted her with his whiskalian glass and sipped the hard liquor while holding her gaze.

Smooth bastard. That's one of the reasons Leopold loved him. Trench could break bones with little effort, but he could sweet talk a woman into his bed with blunt honesty.

"I want you protected with a vanity chip. That's what I meant by modification." Sinner shook his head and rolled his eyes at Trench. "As ironic as it sounds, even though Trench plans to fuck you to death, your safety is our primary goal."

"A man has to have ambition, Sinner." Trench swirled the purple spirits in his glass.

"Trench, you win the prize of being the first to fuck me." Sophia shocked Leopold with that and his drink went down wrong. Choking on his drink, he coughed to get his breath back.

Trench grinned like a man who would devour her. "Yes, I will."

"Fucking hell." Sinner downed his liquor. "Damn sure not the virgin I thought you were."

"Does that disappoint you?" She glanced between the food and Sinner.

"Hell no." Sinner made a face. "Tell me what you have experience with."

Leopold popped a dried dragon-nugget into his mouth. "She's never had her pussy ate."

"Really?" Sinner's eyebrows went up. "Sex without oral sex should be considered a felony in every solar system."

She lifted her fork and pushed the food around.

"Ever suck cock, beautiful?" Sinner pressed, eyeing her like he preferred the meal she offered between her legs.

In all honesty, Leopold preferred that buffet also.

"No." She shook her head. "I'll do it for you guys though if you teach me."

"You're perfect for us." Leopold reached to squeeze her hand.

She smiled at him. "So, tell me what you guys do for a living on Atlantis? Besides murder people."

"I told you I assassinate." Sinner sighed heavily and shook his head. "Assassination is classier."

"Only a born killer would delineate the differences."

"Fair enough." Sinner chuckled at her argument. "I own and operate Atlantis. You could call me the jury and executioner because I preside over all offenses."

"I break bones." Trench winked at her.

Sophia nodded. "So, I have a killer and a bully as my men."

"I'm the bully," Trench said with pride in his voice.

She laughed. "What about you, Leopold?"

"I'm a politician. My father is an intergalactic senator and I'm on the board of the League of Ambassadors. That largely provides me and my family with universal-wide diplomatic immunity. I'm next in line for succession of my father's senator seat."

"That's a nice way of glossing over your crimes." Sinner snorted. "In case you didn't catch the significance of that, it means Leopold—"

"It means," she interrupted Sinner, "that Leopold can ruin lives with impunity."

"Not just sexy, but smart too," Trench said.

Sophia laughed. "Everyone fears you because of the power you have. What can I bring to the table?"

ELEVEN

Sophia

At her question, Trench, Leopold and Sinner shared glances. Sophia interpreted it as they planned to place her in the safe-zone corner.

"Uh uh." She pointed her finger at the duo across from her. "I can't appear weak to your people. You want me safe; I have to present as strong."

"You are strong," Sinner hedged as if he chose his words carefully. "But there's no reason for you to kill, bully, or ruin lives."

He grinned at her as if his words should appease her.

She took turns glaring at each of them. "Fuck that." *Suddenly cursing falls easily from my tongue?* She loved the liberty she felt to express vocally for the first time in her life. "You are all nuts if you think that's going to happen."

"You will *not* talk to me like that, Sophia." Trench's hand fisted on the table.

"I'll talk to you however I want." They stared at one another, his jaw clenched, but she wouldn't back down. She'd never go back to the tongue-biting Sophia again. "I want—no I *demand* to be treated equally. I won't go back to how I lived. Equal or take me back home right now."

"What does it hurt to give her this?" Leopold surprised her when he held his ground against Trench, especially since Trench acted like he governed all one of them. "It's not your decision to make, Trench. This is *her* call."

"Leopold is right. She's right." Sinner shrugged when Trench turned his scowl on him. "We want her safe. I get it, but I won't treat her the same way she's been treated her entire life. Once you get your Neanderthal head on straight, you'll see the wisdom in what we're saying."

Leopold cleared his throat. "What type of badass do you want to be?"

While she considered that question, she stared at Trench and stabbed a chunky piece of yellow food. "I want to learn to fight and shoot a gun."

"We have laser weapons." Sinner brought his utensil to his mouth. "Trench's knife is old-school. He likes to feel it opening flesh."

She looked back at Trench, shivering at Sinner's words. "I'll take whatever weapon I excel at using."

"Fine." Trench said between clenched teeth. "But on two conditions."

"No conditions. This isn't a negotiation."

He ignored her and said, "One… I train you."

She smiled, her core quivering at the idea of his big body manhandling as he taught her to defend herself. "I agree."

"Two... you sit your sexy ass right here." Trench shoved his plate aside and indicated the spot where it'd been. "Spread your legs and allow me to eat your pussy while they dine."

Her pussy vibrated with the idea. She wouldn't turn him down, but she also didn't want to appear weak in front of such strong men either. "What if I decline?"

"Like you said, this isn't a negotiation." Trench sat back in his chair and elevated an eyebrow.

Bluff called; Sophia bit her bottom lip to stop any sound of desperation coming from her. Shoulders tense, arms resting on the arms of his chair, he stared at her. His arrogant attitude implied she'd submit to his request. She wanted his mouth on her pussy, to discover if oral sex was as fantastic as Leopold claimed. If she succumbed to this demand, would they barter for sexual favors on everything?

Eh... would it be so bad if we did?

Mind made up Sophia rose to her feet.

"Before you grant permission, you should know I won't go easy on you." A smirk tilted one side of Trench's mouth. "I'll eat you like you've had my mouth on you a hundred times. I'll push your limits, make you come more than once. You'll have my fingers inside you, deep and fucking you hard. I'll have you coming until you're squirting all over me. Only present yourself if you *think* you can handle that."

With no working knowledge of what he meant by 'squirting', Sophia stared at him and silence lingered in the room. None of them spoke and no one moved. She wasn't even certain anyone breathed.

Trench yawned, but she suspected his indifference was a ruse.

"You might be in over your head, Sophia," Fred startled her when he spoke from behind her.

Heartbeat quickening at her decision, she stepped around behind Leopold's chair and walked about the table. Leopold moved platter and glasses aside as she hopped onto the table in front of Trench.

"Remove your clothes." Trench grasped one of her ankles and set her foot on the arm of the chair.

"Do I push this?" She indicated the same button she'd pressed to make the garment engage.

"Yes." Trench nodded as he placed her other foot on the other arm of the chair.

She glanced at Sinner. His eyes were locked on her.

"Don't look at anyone but me right now." At Trench's words, she shifted her gaze back to him.

Sophia hit the button and the attire vanished. Sinner hissed at her sudden exposure. Unable to glance at him, she couldn't gauge what the hiss implied. Desperate for their approval, she bit her bottom lip as she held Trench's gaze.

Trench slid his hands up the inside of both of her legs. "In case you're questioning Sinner's response, he approves."

"Was that in doubt?" Sinner asked.

"Not to me." Trench spread her legs and scooted forward on his chair. "Lie back with your arms over your head or out to your sides. Leopold don't touch her. I want her senses focused on what I'm doing to her sweet cunt, not on you."

"Fucker," Leopold bitched as her focus met his face. He stood and gave her an upside down kiss.

Even though she wanted to touch Leopold and easily could have grasped his head, she followed Trench's directions and placed her arms out flat on the table.

"I can't wait to discuss the details with you later." Leopold grinned when he lifted his head. "I'm jealous."

Sophia laughed, knowing in that moment he'd become her partner in crime. Trench's fingers touched her, a gentle stroke to her intimate lips. His breath hit her next. She gasped at the strong sensation when his tongue slid through her slit. It felt like every nerve ending in her body came alive. Her fingers tingled and her head buzzed.

"Relax," he said, licking one lip and sucking the other into his mouth. "Let your legs fall open."

Exhaling, she allowed herself to open to him. The vented air kicked in and breezed over her bare skin. She shivered, not because she felt cold but in anticipation of what Trench plotted.

Trust wasn't something she'd ever given to someone before, but she had faith in them to cherish, protect, and eventually love her. They were her men, destined for her.

Trench licked Sophia from ass to her clit

"She's already soaked," Sinner said, admiration pitching his voice at a higher octave.

Trench repeated his move and she whimpered at the shock of pleasure. He circled her clit and in seconds heat spiraled in her belly and ripped through her. Moaning thanks to the quick orgasm, she tried to roll away from his play when he kept flicking at her clitoris.

His protest came in the form of a strong arm circling her thigh and dragging her ass to the edge of the table. Trench set into her, licking and sucking until she cried out with a second climax. His fingers entered her pussy, pushing deep as he plied her sensitive clit with more stimulation.

"Trench!" She would've grasped his hair and pulled him off her, but Leopold pressed her arms back to the table.

Trench growled at her thwarted protest. He fucked her with his fingers deep in her pussy. Sophia gasped when she felt his finger probe her ass, but the way he rubbed his other fingers against her deep inside left her rolling her hips against his palm.

"Oh, god!" Her head rolled from side to side, the sharp sting of him breaching her bottom morphed to create a strange type of pleasure.

Sophia lost herself in the world he transported her to, and she embraced the floaty feeling that enveloped her. Heat circuited her body and she went higher and higher into this new biosphere. Buzzing vibrated her ears, mewls and cries were distant sounds.

Her orgasm hit her broadside without any forewarning.

TWELVE

Trench

One moment Sophia whimpered and moaned in pleasure, and in the next she screamed with her orgasm. Her back arched and her entire body trembled from the magnitude of her pleasure.

"Nanites," Trench muttered against her clit as he fucked her pussy and ass in long strokes of his fingers. She'd tensed when he first pushed his finger into her bottom, and he didn't want her to suffer again. Not that she'd suffered long. The second finger he'd slid into her, she'd taken easier. With her orgasm, she'd drenched him like he'd predicted.

Sinner scrambled from his chair to slam his hand on a panel on the wall. The syringe landed in his palm, and he rushed back to tag her with it. The *whoosh* verified the nanites were delivered.

"I'm surprised she hit subspace that easily." Leopold stared at her in awe.

"Won't take her as long to get there next time." Trench sat back and licked his lips clean of her release.

"She soaked you, Trench." Sinner placed his palm against hers and her fingers curled around his hand.

"I knew she would." Trench lifted her off the table and cuddled her against his chest.

She straddled his thighs, arms limp at her sides, with her face resting in the curve of his neck and shoulder. As he wrapped an arm around her waist, her breathy pants struck his skin and he ran his fingers through her hair.

"Goddamn, that was amazing." Trench grinned at his husbands.

"Fuck yeah it was," Leopold agreed.

Sinner nodded. "I'm so damn hard I hurt."

"Trench?" her voice was raspy.

"Yes, Sophia?" He kissed her temple.

She lifted her head and met his eyes, they remained cloudy from pleasure. "Fuck me." She pulled at Sinner's hand. "All of you fuck me. I need you inside me."

"That's the high talking." Sinner stood and leaned over her, his hand cupping her head. "Give it time to go away."

"I need more. I *need* you. I feel it here." She used her other hand to tap at her chest.

"Do it," Leopold demanded, rising to his feet. "I knew there was something about her purple eyes that was off for her planet. She's a Galinorian."

Shit.

She was more perfect for them than they'd realized.

Trench went to work undoing his pants and she helped him tear at the opening.

Galinorians were a violent female species that populated various galaxies. No one knew how many lived, but they were deadly and skilled at combat. They all had a ravenous hunger for sex, and always had multiple lovers. Once they found their true mates, they would go into a feral state until they had a sexual taste of them. It was like marking their territory.

His cock jerked from his leather pants, eager to reach her. She didn't wait for him to initiate sex. Instead, she grabbed the base of him with her hand and hoisted herself onto his dick.

The head of his dick nestled against her opening. Hot. Wet. Fuck, he couldn't wait to get inside her tight channel.

"Slow down, Sophia." Trench grasped her hips to slow her down. "Don't hurt yourself." Yeah, she was soaked from her orgasms, but he was bigger than the average human male. All of them were.

As a response, she bit his bottom lip and held his gaze as she took all of him in one quick drive downward.

"Holy, fucking hell," he groaned at the tightness of her pussy.

Sophia kissed him. When she pulled back, she rode him like a woman in complete control, taking all of him while her clit scrubbed against his abs.

She is in control.

"Got lube," Sinner said as he reentered the room with a packet in his hand.

Too focused on their woman, Trench hadn't even been aware Sinner left the kitchen.

She smiled up at Leopold and Trench glanced at him to see he stroked his cock, the slit leaking with precum. Without being asked, she leaned toward him and licked the head.

"Oh, that's good, love." Leopold fisted her hair. "Stop moving. Sinner needs you to be still so he can get inside your ass."

"Mmkay." She circled Leopold's crown with her tongue.

"Fuck. That's amazing." The politician moaned as she took him to the back of her throat.

As she sucked Leopold's dick, Trench grasped the cheeks of her ass and spread her for Sinner. The Atlantian owner, slicked up his dick.

Leopold's dick popped from her mouth as she moaned at the press of Sinner into her tight asshole. Through the thin membrane separating them, Trench could feel Sinner's dick pushing into her snug hole.

Her fingernails dug into Trench's shoulders and her eyes went glassy, as she moved one of her hands between their bodies.

"God, woman," Trench muttered as she rubbed her clit hard and attempted an impatient bounce to seat Sinner inside her.

"Stop." Leopold used his fingers in her hair to give her a little yank.

She grinned at Leopold and fell into an orgasm thanks to her masturbation.

"Sweet hell." Trench dropped his forehead against her shoulder as her pussy squeezed about him.

"Fuck it." Sinner thrust all the way inside her ass.

As she came down from yet another orgasm, they worked at fucking her together. As one pushed in, the other pulled out, and Leopold held her head to receive his cock. Sophia grew delirious with pleasure, moaning as they used her the way she desired.

"Can't last." Sinner kissed the side of her neck.

"Me neither." Leopold quickened his plunges into her mouth. She chocked on him, but when he tried to pull back, she reached for him.

Almost simultaneously, Sinner and Trench shoved all the way into her and groaned their releases. Leopold moaned as he shot down her throat. Their climaxes apparently was enough for Sophia to go off again.

THIRTEEN

Sinner

The four of them reclined on their bed. Sophia faced Sinner, her arm throw about his waist, and his leg wedged between hers. Behind her Leopold snuggled against her backside.

Trench wasn't much of a snuggler but since their Olympic sex in the kitchen, they'd taken turns cuddling with her. She'd hit subspace twice and required aftercare. And they enjoyed taking care of her.

"I don't know what came over me," she confessed.

"You're a Galinorian," Leopold said. "Your violet eyes should've clued me in, but the chances of your mother finding your dad on his planet, was slim to none. Very few races visit your solar system."

Sophia rolled onto her back to peer at Leopold. "Why? Are we that awful?"

"No." Trench sat up to look at her. "You're outdated and we don't interfere with the revolution of a world."

"Galinorian women have high sexual drives and almost always have three to five true mates." Sinner used the tip of his finger to circle her bellybutton. "You wanted power, doll, you got it. Galinorians are fierce and skilled warriors. You'll learn quickly once Trench starts to train you."

"Not only that, they're seers," Leopold added.

She made a face. "Seers as in they can see the future?"

"Yes." Leopold nodded. "They're very skilled seers, so your spirit isn't a surprise."

Sophia scrubbed her palms against her face. "So weird. One moment I was basking in the orgasms Trench gave me and in the next I felt like I'd die if I didn't have you all inside me." She lifted her hands. "For the record, oral sex has my nod of approval."

Leopold chuckled. "Mine too."

She blew the politician a kiss.

"Anytime you want me to fuck you with my tongue, come sit that sweet pussy right here," Trench indicated his mouth, "and I'll make you scream."

"I promise to take you up on that offer." Devilry hit her eyes and Sinner wondered what she was thinking.

Knowing her species, she probably plotted world domination or some diabolical shit they'd love.

"Tell me about yourselves," she encouraged. "I want to know everything about your lives."

"Well…" Sinner thought back to his youth. It felt like a lifetime ago. "I was born in a rock mine. My mother died around a year later and I was raised by everyone there."

"He was a scrawny thing when I met him," Trench added, resting against Leopold's back and reaching to touch her stomach.

"You worked in the rock mine too?" She placed her hand over his. "Why were you there? Why would they have children doing this?"

The adorable frown that dug into her forehead demonstrated her inner kindness. Sinner kissed her forehead.

Trench snorted. "My mother sold me to the rock mine to put a roof over her head. I was six when she left me there."

"I was five when Trench showed up." Sinner watched emotions play across her face.

"I hated the work, but I loathed my mother more. She was an abusive crazy bitch who hit often."

Sophia pulled Trench's hand to her mouth and kissed his palm. "That's horrible. I'm so sorry both of you suffered the way you did." She glanced at Sinner to add him to that. "It's not the way children should be treated."

"It's life," Sinner said. "Without the rough upbringing I've no idea how I would've turned out."

Trench shrugged. "It made me strong."

"Turned you into a mean bastard." Sinner grinned.

"That too." Trench chuckled. "I learned a lot in the mines. Things I wouldn't have had the chance to learn without being dumped there. I don't regret my time there and, like I said, I met the first of my twins in that dusty hellhole."

"This showed up immediately when you met him?" Sophia licked the twin flame symbol on Trench's wrist.

"Yes. I'd heard the stories of the legend, but Sinner hadn't." Trench looked at Sinner. "It drew us closer until we became lovers and escaped from that pit."

"That's when they met me." Leopold grabbed her attention.

"We pirated his ship and took him hostage." Trench rubbed his bearded chin against Leopold's shoulder."

"In my prince-like status," Leopold winked at her, "I had an ego the size of a billion universes."

"Had?" Sinner snorted. "He still has a huge ego, doll."

"You would too if your dick was as big as mine," Leopold shot back.

Trench kissed the 'prince's' shoulder. "We can't deny he has the biggest dick of us all."

Sophia laughed.

"These bastards thought they would ransom me back to my father. Then this happened." Leopold showed her his wrist.

"That changed things," she said. "Just like it changed Sinner's plot to kill me."

They sobered.

"Not really." Sinner rolled to his side to face her. "I didn't know you were ours until I got you on the spaceship, Sophia."

"Then why take me?"

"You pulled to something inside me and I made up all sorts of excuses for why I should bring you with me. Near the end I did suspect you were ours, but that wasn't confirmed until I introduced you to them."

Sophia blinked at Sinner. "I came close to dying then."

"Yeah," Sinner admitted.

Trench cleared his throat. "That means we still have someone out there that wants you dead."

"I guess now is the best time to tell you there were two other hits before you."

Anger hit Sinner so fast, his head pounded. He tensed to jump up and start throwing things. Holding back his emotions and calming his internal rage was difficult, but he managed to do it somehow.

"What I know of the Galinorians, they're highly sought. They're captured and sold on the black market all the time." She turned her head to look at Leopold as he spoke, and Sinner went back to watching her face. "I have avenues I can check into, Sinner, because I bet you someone wants her dead because her mother was a black market slave."

Sophia sat up. "You mean you think my dad bought her?"

"I'm not saying that." Leopold shook his head. "She might've escaped from her buyer and found your father. He was powerful on your planet, right?"

She nodded. "Sixth in line for the crown."

"His status would've offered her protection. She could've chosen him, or he could've been her true mate. Are they happily married?"

"My mother died in childbirth."

Leopold reached for her and pulled her back down to lie between them. "We won't allow anyone to harm you."

"I know, but you can't be with me all the time." Her jaw tightened as if she anticipated another argument. "I need to learn to fight immediately."

"Teach her, Trench, and then you two can tag team in the pits," Sinner teased because he knew there wasn't any fucking way any of them wanted to see her in the pits.

"What are the pits?"

"Our man here," Leopold shifted to lie on his back, "Trench is the reigning champion of the fighting pits. Anyone who wants to fight him has to go through all the other champions."

Sophia looked at Trench's knuckles and kissed them. "Why aren't your hands scarred?"

Both corners of Trench's lips ticked upward. "Nanites heal me. We gave them to you earlier so they could heal you when you need it."

"I don't really understand that, but I don't care." She yawned. "I need to sleep."

"I'm glad Sinner found you, Sophia."

She smiled at Leopold. "Me too."

"We'll give you a good life." Leopold kissed her temple. "I promise you that."

FOURTEEN

Sinner

After docking on his reserved spot atop his domain in Atlantis, Sinner strode off the ship to handle a skirmish between two dignitaries of Reddeskii. One of his girls, a whore who was paid well by her johns, had suffered a black eye in the scuffle. It had been accidental, but he didn't give a fuck. Neither did he care who the fuckers were or what role they played on other planets. This was Atlantis. That meant his rules, his punishment. Before guests were allowed to enter the arrival center, they signed waivers to that fact. Fighting had its place on Atlantis, like all vices did, but there was one rule… zero tolerance for breaking the rules.

Because of these assholes, he'd had to leave Sophia with Leopold and Trench when all he wanted to do was welcome her home with his dick inside her. She was a distraction he couldn't allow at the moment.

If these motherfuckers had chosen to solve their differences in the fighting ring, he wouldn't be angry. If they'd scuffled outside of the ring without harming someone else, he wouldn't have been angry either because men would be men. Sinner knew better than anyone they fought to work off their anger. Usually it happened among friends, and they were back to being friends the moment the fists stopped flying. But when one of his workers was injured everything changed.

Activating the vanity chip with a press of a button to his wrist, the biocomputer implanted in his arm altered his appearance. Sinner glanced in the mirrored window and watched as his dark hair shifted to blond and his lithe frame turned pudgy.

Pushing open the door in front of him, he stepped into the cell housing the two men.

Sinner nodded at his man who'd jailed them, and he returned the nod.

"Who the fuck are you?" Dignitary Scrill demanded, not an ounce of regret tattooing his features. "I demanded to see Sinner Prometheus hours ago, not another snot-nosed punk in his organization."

Never wearing the same appearance twice for safety reasons, he understood Scrill's confusion to his identity. Instead of answering the man's insolent question, he pressed his thumb to an area just below his pinkie finger on his palm. Brass knuckles slid into place and he punched the motherfucker in the teeth. Scrill's head whipped backward, and he crashed to the floor with a thud.

"I'm Sinner Prometheus, in case you're still confused, Scrill." He stood over the fallen man, daring him to rise to his feet or give him further attitude.

Blood spilled over Scrill's hand and he moaned. Spitting on the floor, a tooth hit the concrete.

Dignitary Methon scrunched his eyes closed, his mouth moving as if in prayer.

"Don't bother with excuses. The rules were simple. All future visits to Atlantis are revoked. I've a jet ready to return you to your ships immediately." None held the privilege to dock on Atlantis but had to be transported to the planet by jet, a twenty-minute transport. "Show up here again, I won't ask questions, I'll just boot you sorry fuckers into the black hole."

He didn't wait for a confirmation that they understood. Instead he turned on his heel and strode out of the room. Along the way to their residence, he put out a few fires his assistants brought to him. Mostly the businesses ran smoothly, but his reputation at brutality meant the business he'd just settled rarely happened.

A stop at the pharmacy was next. He smiled when he saw Tarot behind the counter.

"Hey, gorgeous." Sinner kissed the woman on her cheek. "The spirits good to you while I was gone?"

"Always, Sinner. I am their mistress."

Never seemed to matter what disguise he wore, Tarot always recognized him. "Anything I need to know?"

Tarot spied for him and let him know when shit was about to hit the fan. "No. I'm following a lead so I might have more tomorrow."

"Let me know."

"Sinner, it's a miracle you've found another twin flame."

He elevated his eyebrows. "You talk to Leopold or Trench?"

"No." She shook her head, the beads in her dark dreadlocks clicking together. "The spirits told me. The one who wants her dead, he's powerful, and he'll send another for her."

"Do you know why he wants her dead?"

"No. Just use every resource you have to protect her."

Sinner nodded. "She's safe on Atlantis."

"Vanity chip for Sophia." Tarot smiled. "You've probably searched a thousand worlds or a hundred-thousand lifetimes for one another, but you've finally come together in this one. It was fate."

He hadn't realized he searched for her until he found her, so what Tarot said made sense to him. "She's special, Tarot. We won't lose her."

"She's a **Galinorian**."

Surprised she saw that much, he gaped at the woman.

Tarot opened a drawer and pulled out a box. "I made this for Sophia this morning. It'll implant the knowledge of our world to her as she sleeps."

"Thanks. Gotta run." He waved and left the pharmacy.

As he zigzagged through the tunnels of his planet beneath the surface, he thought about Sophia, Trench, Leopold and him all together as a cohesive unit. That Tarot saw the danger to

Sophia bothered him. He wanted her safe but knew he could only make her 'safer' because as long as she was associated with them, she'd never be fully protected.

The scanner at his door verified his identity with a blood sample, eye scan, handprint, and voice recognition. It never hurt to be too careful. Only Leopold and Trench possessed the same credentials to enter the room. Anyone else had to be buzzed inside. All cleaning, cooking, and housework was performed by androids, all of which were also imprinted to their DNA.

None of them were naïve enough to believe someone in the galaxy didn't have a hit on their heads. Their planet alone was worth a fortune. Couple that with the business of sin, and that fortune quadrupled.

He entered their dwelling and clicked off his vanity chip. Inside he found their newest twin flame. Sophia stared at one of the androids and touched its face with a finger.

"She feels so real, Fred."

"That's because she's made with synthetic flesh," Sinner said.

Her gaze slid down his body, but he noted her breath quickened. "She's not real, right?"

"She's an android, which is a fancy word for fake person. So, no she's not real." He drew closer and set the pill packet and vanity chip on the coffee table.

Sophia kept staring at the android. "She's amazing. Does she have a name?"

Funny how he saw the joy in the simplest thing

in his life that'd been around for years, all thanks to Sophia. "No, we just call her android."

"We should name her." She looked at him. "Wouldn't it be easier to say, Jess, do whatever? Speaking of," she frowned, "what does she do for you?"

"Everything. She functions as a maid."

"A house servant." Her eyes widened. "I would've loved to have these at home."

"You are home. Where's Leopold and Trench?"

"Leopold's showering. Trench said he'd be back." Grinning, she walked to him and wrapped her arms around his neck. "I didn't mean to imply I wasn't home."

She ruffled her hand through his hair and disappointed him with a quick peck on the lips before sashaying to the window. God, he loved her ass in that catsuit. But he loved her ass best with his dick inside it.

"This view is stunning!"

He tried to see his planet through her eyes, but it was home and nothing new to him.

"The colors are so bright and just beautiful. It's almost magical. I don't think I'll ever get tired of looking at this." She looked over her shoulder at him. "I didn't know some planets had more than one moon."

"D'Skaret has five moons." Leopold emerged from their bedroom butt-ass naked.

"Mmm... that's an even more stunning view," Sophia said as she turned to face Leopold.

The politician executed a naked dance for her,

and she busted out laughing. Sinner smiled at her happiness. They'd given her the peace required to be herself. There was no better feeling than knowing they were to blame for changing her life.

Somethings hadn't changed though. "When Trench gets back, we need to discuss the danger Tarot sees in Sophia's future."

FIFTEEN

Leopold

They'd saved their woman from an assassin, only to discover she wasn't out of danger. Over dinner that night, the four of them sat down to a serious discussion of Sophia's safety. She'd accepted the vanity chip and tried out different looks.

After their meeting, Leopold had called his father to bring him up to date on their new twin and the threat that she was in. His father sent emissaries loyal to their family for centuries to protect her.

She'd explored their home and asked so many questions, she been childlike in her fascination. Sinner had given her the knowledge-pill and she'd swallowed it at dinner, excited to learn all there was to know about Atlantis.

Sinner, Trench, and Leopold caught up on various work-related details while she watched their version of television. It was different from planet to planet, but it was new to Sophia, so she'd been enraptured by it.

When it was time for bed, she strolled ahead of them toward their bedroom and removed her clothes. It was crazy to think how quickly she'd become comfortable around them, but Leopold loved it.

Leopold caught her in the bedroom and turned her into his arms. He trailed the back of his knuckles across her cheek and slid his fingers into her hair. He tightened his hold on her strands to hold her in place but not to sting her scalp.

Watching her face, he leaned into her and brushed their lips together. He took her bottom lip between his teeth and gently tugged, encouraging her to open to him. It got the reaction he wanted. With their mouths sealed together, he lashed his tongue against hers.

Sophia followed his lead without a hint of bashfulness. Her fingers tightened on his neck and he used his hold on her hip to draw her snug against him. She moaned into his mouth and he pulled back.

Her cheeks were flushed, a pretty rosy color against her pale skin. Breathing faster, she touched her lips and stared at him. Eyes wide, a slow smile spread across her mouth.

She turned and went to Trench. The boxer was easy with her, cupping her face and kissing her as deeply as Leopold had. Without hesitation she shifted to Sinner and he pulled her into his arms. With her toes skimming the floor, he kissed the hell out of her.

They came up for air and her puffs were

ragged, gasping sounds. Leopold wished he could see her face because the look on Sinner's was that of a man smitten. When a chick could befall Sinner and Trench, they were fucked. She'd parade them around by their dicks and wield all the power.

Leopold loved that idea.

"I want more." She pushed at Sinner's shirt.

"I'm not sure you're ready for me the way you're moving," Sinner said, halting her hands.

"She's fucking ready." Trench grabbed her about the waist, spun her about and yanked her into his arms. "Have you forgotten so soon how she fucked me on the spaceship?"

Yeah, like a Galinorian out of her mind.

Sophia's legs went around Trench's waist and she buried her hand in his hair. They kissed as he carried her toward the bed.

Trench settled her to sit on the end of the bed and he pulled his clothes off, waiting patiently as Sophia explored his body with her hands. She stroked his dick and rubbed the head against her lips, slicking them with his precum.

With her other hand, she reached for Sin when he removed the last of his clothes. The moment he was within hands reach, she laid her palm on his chest and dragged it down to fondle his hard cock. Both hands full of dicks, she stroked them. Sinner groaned, grabbed her hair and yanked her head back. With his other hand, he wrapped his fingers around hers.

"That touch is nice, but this feels better." Sinner probably tightened her grasp because he preferred a firm grip. Sinner jerked her hand up and down the length of his cock and his hips pumped into her grasp.

She bit her bottom lip and Leopold swore her eyes sparkled. Leopold shucked his clothes as he watched them.

Releasing Sinner, she slid back onto the bed and rested her head on the pillows. She offered herself by spreading her legs.

Trench scrambled over her and found her mouth. Once he lifted his head, he smiled at her and shifted his kisses downward across her neck and collarbone.

"Eat her pussy, Trench." Sinner pushed against Trench's shoulder.

"Yeah, eat my pussy, Trench." She smiled at him and Trench chuckled.

Trench licked his lips and growled, before going down on her.

Sinner sucked on her nipples and used his fingers on them, while Leopold watched. As a voyeur, Leopold spent a lot of time watching Sinner and Trench do each other. That was when he wasn't sandwiched between them.

"Oh my god, that feels good," she whispered.

SIXTEEN

Trench

Her breath stuttered from her, as her hips rocked toward Trench's mouth. He applied one last lick to her clit before he shifted from between her legs. "Leopold, get your ass over here."

Trench sat beside her as he reached for Leopold. He kissed the politician as Sinner stuffed himself on her pussy. Trench focused on Leopold, stroking his cock and biting on his nipples, as Sinner got Sophia ready for them.

He knew the moment she came because of the soft cry that left her lungs.

Trench and Leopold watched Sophia and Sinner, as Sinner rose over her. The Atlantis' leader, palmed her neck and clamped his fingers on her jaw. Their gazes locked as she panted in the aftermath of her climax and Sinner positioned his hips between her thighs, spreading her with his knees. When he jerked his hips forward, she arched beneath him with a gasp.

Sinner fucked her in long strokes. Trench used Leopold's distraction to lean down and suck his cock.

"Fuck!" Leopold exclaimed when Trench sucked him into his mouth.

He curled his tongue along the underside of Leopold's cock to drag upward and rope around his crown to tease the slit. Leopold grasped Trench's head and fucked into his mouth. Trench used his hand to cup and knead Leopold's balls, while taking his hard length down his throat. Trench swallowed and Leopold shot off. But much like a Galinorian a Ragaran was just getting started after the first climax.

"Your turn." Leopold kissed Trench. "Sinner, I want her ass."

Leopold grabbed a bottle of lube while Sinner rolled so she was on top. Sophia sat up and rode Sinner. She was so fucking hot with her blonde hair flowing around her while she took Sinner.

Trench grabbed her head and kissed her while she fucked Sinner. She groaned into his mouth and he bet Leopold used his fingers to lube up her backside. Galinorians were nearly insatiable creatures, and she'd done her best to prove that myth as the truth.

Leopold used his hand on the back of her neck to push her down onto Sinner's chest. Sinner helped him by grabbing the cheeks of her ass and pulling them apart, exposing her tiny little rosebud. Leopold blew a kiss at Trench and lined the fat head of his dick up with her ass. Trench's cock pulsed with the idea of Sophia taking

Leopold thickness, while he envied Sinner getting to feel Leopold's dick against his.

"Oh, my!" She whimpered as Leopold pushed into her bottom.

She kissed Sinner as Leopold went deeper, until he was seated all the way inside her, with his balls hanging against her pussy and Sinner's cock.

"Do you need a second, Sophia?" Leopold pointed at Trench's cock. "Stand so I can suck your dick while I fuck her."

"No," Sophia panted against Sinner's mouth. "Fuck me."

Leopold and Sinner needed no further provocation but worked in unison together to bring her the greatest pleasure. Trench used Leopold's mouth and throat to fuck, while Leopold sucked on him and fucked her.

"You're ours, baby," Sinner said, "we'll protect you because you're the most precious thing in our lives."

Trench couldn't last any longer and shot down Leopold's throat. A few moments later Sinner, went off, but Leopold kept going, driving into her tight ass. Leopold shoved deep and rolled her off Sinner and onto her side. He clasped her knee and pulled it upward, so Trench and Sinner had a bird's eye view of him fucking that sweet ass.

Sophia came and Leopold moaned at her release, but he kept going, giving her hard thrusts.

"Look at Trench and Sinner," Leopold commanded against her ear as he kept shoving into her.

Her eyes lifted to them and whatever she saw on their faces had her mouth parting and her eyes widening. Sophia's breathing grew heavy and ragged.

"Rub your clit and come again while they watch you get your ass fucked hard." Leopold went up on his forearm, adjusted her so that her leg hooked over the back of his thighs, and he wrapped his fingers around her hip.

Her eyes glazed over as Leopold fucked her like a goddamn maniac, her breathing was nothing but choppy gasps of air. When her fingers touched her swollen clit, a squeal left her lungs. In no more than a minute she cried out and her hand fell away, as her body shivered with her orgasm. Trench was in awe over the pleasure on her face as her body shook from her climax.

Sinner moved quickly to rub her clit and extend her enjoyment. Trench shifted to join him, shoving two fingers inside her cunt. He found the spongy area high in her pussy and gave it the attention it needed. Another two, three minutes and she came again, squeezing his fingers while she squirted over his hand.

Leopold gave into his own bliss, shoved deep and groaned as he came. No one moved for a few moments. When Trench slid his fingers from her pussy, she whimpered. With Leopold still buried in her ass, the three of them snuggled together in a tangle of limbs.

SEVENTEEN

Sophia

Sophia woke sometime later with the moon still in the sky. She couldn't believe she could fuck her men as hard as she did and not be sore. But so far, she hadn't felt a twinge of pain.

On her left was Trench, with Sinner at his back. Thanks to the purple glow of the moon shining through the window, she could see that Sinner's arm circled Trench's waist and Sinner snuggled against his back. She lay on her side facing them, loving the softness of their features in sleep. Behind her Leopold snuggled against her back and his arm rested on her hip. She'd fallen asleep with his big cock inside her ass.

How in the hell she took him, she'd never know, when he was thicker and longer than the other two of her men. But he'd felt just as great as Sinner and Trench had when they'd fucked her.

Her head lay on Leopold's bicep, using him as a pillow, while the shallow puffs of his breath against her ear soothed her.

As lovers they were intense, and she loved every second of intimacy with them.

Being herself was liberating. In her world, she would've never dreamed to take on three men at once. Despite the irony that even married men had mistresses, on Uriel she would've been labeled a whore had society even thought there was an appearance of impropriety.

Leopold, Trench, and Sinner didn't make her feel anything but beautiful and, even though they hadn't said the words, she felt loved. Adored even.

Inching from Leopold's hold, she wiggled down the mattress to climb off the bed.

"You shouldn't be here," she hissed low at Fred when she saw him standing near the window.

"I'm always with you." He didn't look at her but stared out the window. "I've never seen this world. It's beautiful."

She smiled. "Yes, it is."

Two purple moons hung in the sky. One of them was so close it looked as if she could reach out and touch the bright lavender pockmarked terrain. The indentions or craters on its surface were as visible as the body of water to the left and below her. The unique glow the moons made on the water was beautiful, a mixture of dark purple to lilac. Their radiance made everything appear softer, more serene with a tint of soft violet. The second moon was further away, a paler purple, but just as beautiful.

"You're happy?" Fred faced her.

"Yes." She looked over her shoulder at the three men sleeping on the bed. "Even though you told me I'd have more than one lover, I never truly understood the dynamics until now."

Fred chuckled. "You wanted adventure because you knew you didn't belong on your world."

"Who you talking to, love?"

She looked toward the bed as Leopold sat up and rubbed the sleep from his face with a hand before sending it on an upward swipe through his hair.

"Fred."

"Hmm..." He stood and walked toward her, his nudity a thing of beauty in the soft glow of the moons.

His cock was pierced in a ladder of steel along the top and through his crown. Likewise, his nipples, tongue and ears all had been pierced. According to him it was a common custom among his race and often times parents had their children pierced at birth. Each year they added a new piercing to the dick. If the tradition was followed to the letter, they didn't stop adding to them until their twentieth year of life when they were considered a man.

Leopold had all twenty steel bars and he'd added the one through his crown to signify his royal heritage because only royalty were allowed that piercing. His piercings created a ribbed feeling when he was inside her, a dynamic that gave her intense pleasure.

She hadn't even known such a thing existed.

Leopold drew her to him and gave her a chaste kiss. "Was your ghost, Fred, pervy? Did he watch us?"

She turned to her spirit guide. "Did you?"

Fred's smile served as a reply.

"Yeah," she confirmed and shook her head.

"I'm just a man," Fred argued. "Have to get my jollies where I can."

"You're a ghost." She rolled her eyes. "You shouldn't have jollies."

Leopold laughed. "Let me guess, he's defending why he watched?"

"Bingo," Fred said.

"Oh, so you *can* hear him?" She grinned.

"Nah… spirit or not, he's a guy." Leopold kissed her forehead.

"Told you," her ghost mocked her.

"All men are perverts." With his palm under her chin, he tipped her head back and kissed her.

Sophia moaned into him, growing aroused despite all the orgasms she'd enjoyed earlier. When they touched her, she ignited. It was wonderful and terrifying, and she wouldn't change a thing.

"I want to fuck you up against the window." He kissed across her cheek, down her jaw and along her neck. Against her ear, he whispered, "Will you let me?"

"Yes," she said, breathy and already wet.

"Tell me if it hurts and I'll stop." Using his hands on the bottom of her ass, he lifted her and put her back to the window.

SOPHIA'S CONNECTION

Sophia wrapped her legs around his waist as he hooked her a bit higher and the tip of his dick prodded against her pussy opening. He halted and stared into her eyes as he slowly lowered her onto his fat, pierced cock.

"Oh, my goodness, why doesn't this get old?" As he thrust into her in a slow rock, she didn't expect an answer to her question.

"Because you're mine, meant for me." He growled, with his golden eyes glowing. She'd noticed any time he was inside her, his eyes glowed. It had to be a Ragaran thing.

"She's ours," Trench said from behind Leopold.

"She's meant for *us*," Sinner muttered as he stopped to stand beside her. "Put her on her feet and turn her toward the window so she can look at her new world while *I* finish her off and Trench finishes you."

"Tell them to fuck off, Sophia," Leopold glared at Sinner.

Intrigued because she wanted to watch her men together, she asked, "Will Trench fuck you or suck you off?"

"Fuck him," Trench said.

Her channel clenched at the idea.

Leopold's head turned and he met her gaze. "That excites you?"

"Yes, very much."

Smiling, he kissed her again before lifting her off his cock and setting her on her feet. "Your wish is my pleasure to grant."

On the tip of her tongue were the words, "I

love you," but she bit them back. "You're the best," she said instead.

Trench kissed Leopold and she sighed at the way they moved together, anticipating the other one's moves. They were a well-oiled machine and she knew in time she'd be that way with the three of them.

"Face the window, doll," Sinner instructed.

She looked up at him before following his instructions. He grasped her hips and pulled her a few steps backward. Once he had her where he wanted her, he pushed against her shoulder blades and she leaned forward. She planted her hands on the window to stabilize herself in the half-bent position.

Sinner knocked his foot in between her feet until her stance was the way he desired. He caressed the head of his cock through her folds. "Leopold already has you so very wet."

"You all have me wet." She looked to her left to find Leopold in the same position as her with Trench lubing him up.

Leopold reached for her hand and she moved her hand closer to his. They laced their pinkie fingers together on the window. He held her eyes as Trench pushed into him, and he groaned when Trench was seated deep, his eyes so golden they glimmered in the purple glow of the moons.

"Does he feel good, Leopold?" she asked.

"Yes," his voice was gruff with enjoyment.

Trench grabbed his hips and pulled him back into his cock as he thrust into Leopold. She looked back at Leopold's face, loving the glowing sheen of his silver-blue marks of his skin. Sinner pushed deep into Sophia, barely giving her time to adapt to his penetration. As they enjoyed the cocks of their men, hers and Leopold's hands moved to clasp, their fingers interlaced. Leopold's other hand yanked along his dick as heat curled through her loins.

When she came, Sinner pulled out and thrust into her backside before she could come down from her high. The pleasure was so intense, she whimpered and braced her forearms on the glass while she received Sinner anally.

"You're beautiful when you come," Leopold muttered, squeezing her hand.

She smiled at him, her whimpers falling from her lungs as she drifted into that buzzy world they always sent her.

EIGHTEEN

Sinner

Sophia put Trench on his ass.

The thud of his big body hitting the dojo mats echoed in the room.

Proud of her accomplishment, she crowed her win with a cheering noise. "The crowd is in her corner and they cheer at her victory."

Leopold whooped her victory, egging her on.

Sinner grinned at their antics.

Trench came off the mat slow. "I said be gentle."

"You stepped into the move, providing your weight for the throw. It's your fault you hit the mat hard, you big baby." She taunted him by making a 'come here' motion with her hands.

"I'm going to spank you for that." Trench never made a promise he couldn't keep. "Make you come while I apply my hand to your backside."

Sinner knew her well enough he could practically see her pussy plumping up and growing wet at Trench's promise.

SOPHIA'S CONNECTION

"How's punishing me fair?" Her hands hit her hips. "You want me to kick ass, but you're going to punish me for kicking *your* ass? *Tsk... tsk...*" Sophia shook her head as she circled him. "How about this deal. You lose, I spank your tight ass until you come."

"I don't like being spanked," Trench countered, following her with his gaze.

"You will if Leo is sucking your dick while I do it."

Checkmate.

Sinner laughed at her counter.

"What are you laughing at, Sinner?" Trench scowled in his direction.

"I'll up the ante, Sophia." Sinner elevated his eyebrows to challenge Trench. "Beat him, and you can spank him while Leo sucks his dick. Once your arm is tired, I'll fuck him until he blows down Leo's throat."

"No," Trench said at the same time she said, "I get to video so we can watch it later on the big screen."

Trench shook his head. "That you're ganging up on me isn't fair."

"Now who is bitching about fairness?" Leopold prodded. "I'll make an even better deal. You win, Sophia, and I'll give you a strap-on to fuck Trench with."

Her eyes lit up. "Oooo... I take that option."

"I never agreed." Trench pouted.

Three months into their relationship Sophia excelled and changed more than Sinner could've imagined. She learned fast and enjoyed the combat skills Trench taught her. Keeping her safe remained at the top of their priorities.

Sinner had people working on who hired him to assassinate Sophia, but not a single source revealed the culprit because no one knew anything to divulge. Weird how someone could put a hit on his twin flame and not one lead pointed to a particular person.

The job request bounced around more than a few internet universes making it untraceable to even the most skilled hacker. Sinner remained on guard, implemented extra security measures, welcomed the emissaries Leopold's dad sent, and they taught her self-defense skillsets just in case. She already mastered shooting a blaster. If it wasn't sexy enough that she wore it strapped to her hip all the time, she also owned a pocket laser that could cut through anything, including steel, making human flesh as easy as butter.

"I think Trench needs a lesson in humility." Sinner stepped in behind Trench and commanded, "Remove your pants and get on your knees."

"No." Trench turned his head and stared at Sinner over his shoulder. "Sophia likes her ass spanked. I don't."

Sinner placed a hand on Trench's shoulder. "You're getting fucked."

Trench's eyes widened. He rarely received.

"By Sophia." Sinner met Trench's stare dead-on. "Leopold."

When Sinner uttered Leopold's name, he ran across the room while Sophia halted in front of Trench and frowned.

"Don't worry, big guy, I'll be gentle with you." She kissed his chest and Trench grasped her head.

Leopold entered the room and held up a purple, thick and veiny strap-on. It was big enough it would've given Sinner pause.

She squealed at the sight of the sexy toy. "They're giving me a dick, Trench."

Leopold chuckled and Sinner grinned. Three months ago, she wouldn't have uttered the word dick.

Sophia's eyes glowed with excitement.

Trench groaned.

Her gaze flashed to Trench, hesitation killing her fleeting anticipation. "You don't want me to, I won't." She went onto her tiptoes and kissed him. "Let's get back to lessons." She set the toy aside. "So what move am I learning now?"

She stepped back, but Trench reached for her and drew her to him. "How to top me."

"Yes!" Leopold let loose a fist-pump into the air.

No one would ever top Trench, not fully. If anyone stood a chance, though, it was Sophia. They all loved her, adored her, and lived to see that she was happy.

"Get naked," Sinner said. "Both of you."

Leopold grabbed the strap-on and showed it in more detail to Sophia. "This part goes inside you." He indicated the second cock. "It vibrates. Can you hold off your climax long enough for Trench to come first?"

Leo pressed a button and both fake-cocks

vibrated.

"This area here," Sinner reached out and ran his finger along the ridged top of the inner dildo, "will vibrate against your clit and g-spot while you fuck Trench."

Sophia's breath quickened.

Trench chuckled. "I bet I last longer than you."

"I bet you do too." She stripped off her clothes, slow enough it whet all their appetites. "Bet I can come more than you though."

Trench groaned this time. "Bet you can too."

"Either way," she bit Trench's bottom lip, "it's a win-win for me, just like having you three as my twin flames is a win-win."

"For us too." Trench growled and kissed her, plunging his tongue into her mouth.

Sinner chuckled at Trench's inability to be topped. Some things never changed.

Sophia gasped and her eyes went wide. She shoved away from Trench and looked at her arms. "What is wrong with me?"

She moaned in pain. Movement beneath her arms showed the nanites in her system creating pinpricks beneath her skin. She smacked at her arms, but the technology continued to gyrate.

Sinner's pulse escalated and he could hear his heartbeat in his ears. Black spots flashed in his vision and a wave of dizziness threatened to put him on his ass. Then everything slowed down and came into focus. He reacted.

He grabbed her in his arms, a cold sweat had turned her face ashen. She clasped at his arms, her fingertips digging into his muscles.

SOPHIA'S CONNECTION

She gasped for breath and jerked in his arms. "C-can't b-b-breathe," she choked out as the white of her eyes showed.

His best guess was her nanites worked to kill her.

"I'm sorry." He pressed his wrist to her neck and executed an electrical zap to kill the technology for now.

Sophia pulsed from the shock and went limp in his arms. Before Sinner could swing her into his arms, Trench yanked her from Sinner's grasp and clutched her to the boxer's massive chest.

"Motherfuck," Leopold snarled. "Someone hacked her goddamn nanites in an attempt to kill her."

"That's what I surmised too." Sinner watched Trench kiss Sophia's face while he snuggled her in his protective arms.

The hardass in their group had lost his shit. When Trench returned to his senses, he'd want blood as much as Sinner and Leopold did.

"They'd have to be in close range." Leopold took off at a dead run.

Sinner initiated 'lock down' protocol on his arm device. No ship or person would be able to exit his planet. He had faith in Leopold's abilities and connections. Once they found the would-be assassin, they *would* get any information they had from the bastard.

NINETEEN

Sophia

Head and chest aching, Sophia pressed her fist between her breasts and rubbed at her temples with the fingers of her other hand. Wincing because she ached everywhere, she flexed her fingers to drive away the pain, but the discomfort remained.

It tasted like something died in her mouth and her throat felt like hot desert sand. She tried to swallow, but that hurt too.

"Easy. Drink this." Jess, the name Sophia had given the android, leaned over and came into her view.

Next to her stood Fred. "Let's not do that again."

Like she had something to do with how she felt. Sophia rolled her eyes at him and, ignoring the aches, she wanted to soothe her parched throat before she asked Fred questions. She grabbed the glass Jess offered and gulped the water. She choked on the cool liquid as it burned her throat. Jess plucked the glass from Sophia's hand and waited for her to catch her breath.

Her guys walked into the room, their steps heavy and quick. Joy at having them near surged inside, making her heartbeat escalate and her stomach executed a little butterfly-roll.

"What happened?" she croaked out, admiring their sexy swaggers.

"Another assassination attempt." Sinner said from the foot of the bed. "The nanites meant to protect you were hacked to attack you. Smart move actually."

As she processed his words, she held Sinner's gaze.

Leopold sat beside her and pulled her back against his chest. "Scared the fuck out of us."

Wearing a scowl, Sinner looked more pissed off than impressed. "How do you feel?"

"Like someone tried to kill me." She had been frightened too. The way those nanites had turned against her not only hurt like a mofo but she was still sore from the attack. "How long was I out?"

"A little over twenty-four hours." Trench brooded like always, his scowl biting into his forehead.

Worlds away from her home planet, Sophia had felt safe on Atlantis with her three tough guys. No one defied them without consequences, so she'd been protected from her former dangers. Or so she'd thought.

A coldness seeped into her limbs and she shivered at how close she'd come to dying. If they couldn't save her, who could?

Trench climbed onto the bed to cuddle up

beside her. His arm circled her stomach as he aligned against her side and his head rested on her stomach. She slid her fingers across his massive arms, loving the feel of his muscles.

Normally his larger than life presence and warmth eased any distress she felt, and left her snuggly in his warmth, but the hit had come from the inside out. Literally. An army of tough guys couldn't battle technological assaults.

Well, maybe they could because Sinner had knocked her out with whatever he'd done to her. And she *was* alive, so they'd been able to combat the strike somehow.

"We caught the motherfucker," Trench said against her ear. "We really need you to drink the water too because there are new nanites in it to heal you and flush the traitors out of your body.

Trench's hair was unbraided today, and his hair flowed about his shoulders. She slid her fingers through the dark strands. Trench shimmied upward to lean against the headboard and snuggle even closer to her.

Sophia's big, bad, tough bully gave her a platonic kiss. To comfort her or himself, she wasn't sure. Either way, she *loved* his gentle side. He didn't show it often, and usually it only came out for her.

"It was a robot assassin. We dismantled it after we got the information we sought." Sinner placed a knee on the end of the bed, drawing her attention back to him. "We've already retrieved the bastard that wants you dead. I identified him as Lord Helms."

SOPHIA'S CONNECTION

"Lord Helms from my planet? *That* Lord Helms?" Lord Helms had come from the North with a hefty bank account and a documented heritage of fine aristocracy. Without much of an inquiry, the noble peerage had accepted him with open arms.

Less than a month after his introduction to polite society, Lord Helms had asked her father for her hand in marriage. Her father had thought it a suitable match, but Sophia had declined. Her parent hadn't seemed surprised by her rejection, but she had spurned many would-be suitors. She'd cited a lack of attraction to Lord Helms, but in truth he'd made her skin crawl with the way he leered at her. It was bad enough she was forced to stomach his presence at gatherings, but intimacy would've been impossible with him.

"Yeah," Sinner confirmed. "That Lord Helms."

"He wasn't from Uriel?"

Sinner shook his head. "He's from Grid, a planet where their people are half android and half humanoid. I asked why he wanted you dead. He said if he couldn't have you then no one else could either."

Leopold's fingers slid through her hair. "My father discovered he was banished from Grid for claiming brides against their will. He already has seven wives."

Trench snorted and kissed her bare shoulder. "He doesn't realize our bride requires more than one man to satisfy her particular needs."

Sophia licked her lips and reached for the glass

of water Jess held. Sitting forward to drink the water a little easier, one of the guys behind her slid his fingers up and down her spine. Naked, bare skin on bare skin, sent a message to her lady bits and her insides went hot and gooey.

Of course, Trench wasn't wrong either. She'd researched her ancestry and discovered everything they told her was true. Galinorian women always had multiple husbands because their sexual appetites exceeded that of most men. She wondered how that had worked with her parents but had come to the conclusion she'd never know.

"I told you something was off with Lord Helms," Fred muttered as he paced the room. "I knew something felt mechanical about him. Sorry I let you down, Sophia."

"You did your best, Fred. I've never asked for more." That none of her guys blinked at her reply to Fred indicated how they'd become accustomed to her chatter with her spirit guide.

"What'd Fred say?" Leopold asked.

"Just that he knew Lord Helms felt mechanical. Fred knew there was something off about him and warned me. Lord Helms also gave me the creepy-crawlies." Sophia sipped on the water, forcing it down her burning throat in small swallows. As she ingested nanites, they'd heal her and make it easier to swallow.

Lord Helms had looked normal to her eyes, like any other man, and he'd been pleasing on the eyes. His behavior had been what unsettled her. That Fred had been unable to get a definitive read on him had alarmed her as well. "Is Lord Helms still alive?"

"Yeah." Sinner nodded.

"I want to talk to him." Sophia wanted to look Lord Helms dead in the eye and confront him. It was a burning need inside her.

Sinner grinned and glanced between Trench and Leopold. "I told you both she'd want to see him."

"Don't gloat," Trench growled.

"It's not attractive," Leopold added.

Sophia blew him a kiss. "It's very attractive."

Realizing the nanites had begun to work, she downed the last of the water, thankful that swallowing created nothing but a dull ache now. Crawling off the bed, she strode across the room and placed her palm on a panel on the wall. Funny how she'd grown comfortable with the new tech their world offered.

On the wall, a screen lit up and she selected the color red for blood and a catsuit design because it was comfy. A door opened revealing a tiny swatch of what she would call material, but it was made from something her planet didn't have. Placing it on her wrist the stuff activated and dressed her in a pantsuit. An offering of accessories slid from another panel in the wall and she selected a blingy, rhinestone belt to go about her waist.

Trench growled. "I love you in red."

"I prefer you naked." Leopold strode to her and kissed her cheek.

She laughed at Leopold, remembering their

first meeting when he'd told her she wore too many clothes and asked her if she wanted to get naked. "I'm ready to face Lord Helms."

Sinner offered her his hand and she laced her finger with his. "Lord Helms' real name is Gerekel of House Clozen. They're not a surname type of planet."

Sophia would *never* use his real name because that would acknowledge his true identity. She wanted him to know she never saw him as more than what he presented himself to her. A fraud, a monster, and just another man who wanted to take her will away.

Sinner guided her out of their home with Trench and Leopold following behind. The presence of her guys gave her confidence because she knew they'd have her back in any situation. They'd die before they allowed her to die. Thanks to them, she possessed skill to hold her own against most any foe.

They halted at a door and Sinner looked at her. "You ready?"

She squeezed his hand. "Yes."

He leaned in for an eye scan and the door slid open. The brown-haired man she'd known as Lord Helms stood in the corner of the room with his arms crossed over his chest. He glared toward the door.

The moment he spotted her, he came out of his lounging position and his scowl evaporated. He came toward her. "Sophia, my beautiful darling."

"Stay back." Trench put himself between her and Lord Helms. The fraud of a man glared at

Trench. "I'd like nothing better than to snap your neck. My bride wishes to speak with you before I do that."

Helms' gaze shot to her and his eyes narrowed. "You married this scum?"

"I'm married to all three of them." Technically speaking they weren't "married" through her custom, but she considered herself wedded to them.

"That makes you a whore." He spat on the ground. "Not fit to be my bride."

"Motherfucker—"

"Sit down, Trench," she cut him off before he got wound up.

Trench met her eyes with a clenched jaw. He nodded and backed down, but he ignored the seat she requested he take. Instead he stepped to her back and stood so that she could feel his heat. She bet he glowered at Helms so he wouldn't forget who protected her.

Sinner grabbed a chair, spun it around and straddled the seat. He rested his forearms on the top of the back. Leopold took up the space on the opposite side of her with his arms crossed over his beautiful chest. That left her with a man on either side and one at her back. The one facing her wasn't a man in her eyes, but a monster.

"I didn't want to be your bride." She wouldn't quibble over him having seven wives, therefore making him an even bigger whore. "I wanted to look you in the eyes, and have you explain to me why you wanted me dead. Now that I'm here, I don't care. It's because of *you* that I found my men. And they're all that matter to me. Thank you for the gift you've given me. Without your vile, pettiness I would've never found them, so thank you for the amazing life you've given me."

Grabbing Trench's hand, she pulled him toward the door. "You're through?"

"Yeah." The door slid open and she tugged him from the cell. "He's not important after all."

"Can I kill him now?" Sinner asked as he and Leopold exited the room and the door slid shut behind them.

"How will you do it?" She looked up at Sinner, loving everything about him.

"We put nanites in his body. When I push this button"—he fiddled with the implant beneath his wrist and a purple light flashed beneath his arm—"they'll activate and kill him the same way he planned to kill you."

A reasonable ending for the monster who wanted her dead for no other reason than he couldn't have her. Sophia touched the purple button on Sinner's arm.

"*Sophia.*" The higher pitched tenor of Sinner's voice detailed his surprise.

"That's my blood thirsty girl." Leopold grinned and kissed her.

She clasped his face and looked up at him. "I love you, Leopold."

"Love, I love you too."

She hooked her fingers through Sinner's belt loops and went onto her tiptoes to brush her lips against his. As she met his eyes, she said, "I love you, Sinner. Thank you for flying across galaxies to kill me."

He chuckled against her lips. "It has turned into one of the greatest moments of my life." Sinner's hand palmed the back of her head and he slid his tongue between her lips to give her a hell of a smooch. "Just in case you didn't already know, I love you."

Trench yanked her from Sinner's hold and turned her to face him.

"You love me. I know. I love you as well, you hellion." Trench lifted Sophia and she squealed at the sudden upending. He dropped her over his shoulder and popped her ass. "We almost lost you. *I need to fuck you.* I *need* to be inside you, feel you clenching my dick as you come undone around me."

She smacked his ass as he begin to stride along the hall, but her blows didn't slow his pace. A minute later he dropped her on their bed. The wild glaze in his eyes let her know how much her near-death experience had impacted him.

"I can tell you, from experience, *that* look on his face," Leopold said, "means it's going to be a long night of pleasure."

"After this, you might want to almost die a couple of times a week." Sinner stripped.

Trench dropped on the bed beside her, flat on his back. "Undress and put your pussy right here." He licked his lips to indicate the spot.

Sophia rolled on top of him and clasped his face between her hands. "I love you and all your intensity. Don't ever change, Trench."

"You four are at it again?" Fred groaned. "This

porno is getting old. I'm covering my eyes."

For the first time in a long time Sophia faced the future with optimism and excitement. Boring would no longer be in her vocabulary. "Where's the strap-on you guys gave me?"

Trench groaned. "No."

"Got it right here." Leopold stood beside the bed with the sex toy in his hand.

"Not tonight," Trench said again. "You're going to think you've died and gone to the afterlife before I'm finished with you."

Sophia threw her strip of cloth over the side of the bed and straddled Trench's face in reverse cowgirl style. "Shut up and eat me, Trench." She leaned over and took his cock in her grasp, his balls in her other hand. "If I make you come first, I get to fuck you with the dildo."

He groaned but tugged her to his mouth and went to work.

Sophia moaned, and gave him a run for the challenge.

In the end, everyone was a winner.

OTHER BOOKS BY GRACEN

The Private Dick series
(co-authored with Julie Morgan)

Dick (#1)

The Drakki Chronicles
(Black Hollow series)

Finding Her Fire

**Hot Wired series
(rock star romance)**

Rockin' the Heart
Lost in the Beat
Bama Girl Blues
Sugar Ink Serenade

Siren Song series

Kissing Sassy
Sassy Vigilante
Sassy Bride

Grim Riders series

Ghost
Jedi

Stand Alone Romance/Erotic Romance

Fairy Casanova
Taboo Kisses
Demon Spelled
Elfin Blood

Lie to Me
Sexy in Hot Pink

Reaped
(co-authored with Tina Carreiro)

A Twin Flame Novel
Celia's Connection
Sophia's Connection

The Road to Hell series
(paranormal romance)

Madison's Life Lessons (prequel)
Pandora's Box (# 1)
Hell's Phoenix (# 2)
Genesis Queen (# 3)
Royal Partnerships (# 4)

ABOUT GRACEN

GRACEN MILLER is a hopeless daydreamer masquerading as a "normal" person in southern society. When not writing, she's a full-time lacrosse mom for her two sons and a devoted wife to her real-life hero-husband of over twenty-five years. She has an unusual relationship with her muse, Dom, but credits all her creative success to his brilliant mind. She's addicted to writing, paranormal romance novels, horror movies, Alabama football, and coffee... addictions are not necessarily in order of priority. She's convinced coffee is nectar from the gods and when blending coffee and writing together it generates the perfect creative merger. Many of her creative worlds are spawned from coffee highs and Dom's aggressive demands. Gracen writes is multiple genres—paranormal romance, paranormal eroti romance, rock star contemporary romance, and dystopian romance. To learn more about Gracen or to leave her a comment, visit her website at www.gracen-miller.com.

Made in the USA
Columbia, SC
10 July 2023